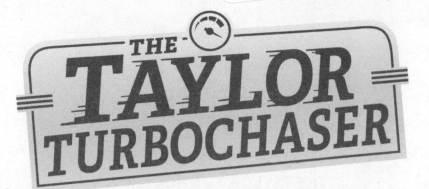

THE TAYLOR TURBOCHASER

Books by David Baddiel

ANIMALCOLM

BIRTHDAY BOY

HEAD KID

THE PARENT AGENCY

THE PERSON CONTROLLER

THE TAYLOR TURBOCHASER

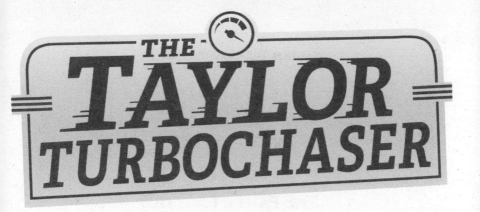

DAVID BADDIEL

Illustrated by Steven Lenton

HarperCollins *Children's Books*

First published in Great Britain by
HarperCollins *Children's Books* in 2019
HarperCollins *Children's Books* is a division of HarperCollins*Publishers* Ltd,
HarperCollins Publishers
1 London Bridge Street
London SE1 9GF

The HarperCollins website address is
www.harpercollins.co.uk

1

HB ISBN 978–0–00–833415–4
TPB ISBN 978–0–00–833416–1
SPECIAL EDITION ISBN 978–0–00–838022–9
SPECIAL EDITION ISBN 978–0–00–838281–0

Typeset in ITC Novarese 12/22pt
Printed and bound in England by CPI Group (UK) Ltd, Croydon, CR0 4YY
A CIP catalogue record for this title is available from the British Library.

To Morwenna

The Bit Before
the Beginning

Amy Taylor *loved* cars. Here are her favourite ones:

1. ***The Aston Martin DB5.*** This is the one James Bond drives. Amy just loved the look of this one. Although as with all old cars (classic cars, as people in the know – like Amy – call them) if she had one she would get someone to remake it with an

electric engine, so that it wasn't bad for the planet. Maybe with the help of her friend Rahul, who was an inventor. Of sorts.

2. ***The Mercedes 300 SL Gullwing***. This was another classic car. But it had doors that instead of opening normally came up like

wings, making the whole car look like it could fly. It couldn't.

3. ***The Jaguar E-Type,*** which was also an old car, but she liked the new one, called the Zero, which was actually electric. It was

just as beautiful as the old car, and Amy thought it was very clever that the car had always been called the E-Type, even before there was an electric version.

4. **The Ford Transit Van.** Well, *a* Ford Transit van. Her mum's white battered seven-year-old one.

Amy's love for cars might seem unusual. Not because she was a girl – lots of girls like cars and lots of boys don't – but because she had been in a really bad car accident when she was eight years old. Which also meant that since then – she was now eleven – she had needed to use a wheelchair.

Amy's accident was also why the Ford Transit van was on her list of favourite cars. As a petrolhead – that's slang for car fan – she knew it wasn't up there with the Aston Martin and the Gullwing, but she also knew that her mum had spent a lot of time and money converting this old a-bit-like-Mater-from-*Cars* wagon into something that could transport Amy and her chair (and her very, *very* teenage-boy brother Jack – you'll meet him in a bit). This made the van one of a million reasons why Amy loved her mum. She often felt an *especially* huge love for her mum as she easily wheeled her chair up the ramp that came out of the back of the van.

"Thanks, Mum!" she'd say, as she rolled up into the back of the Transit. "Look! I can do it one-handed . . . !"

Actually that isn't true.

Or rather: it isn't true *any longer*.

Amy *used* to be able to wheel her way easily up the ramp into the van, but not any more. The problem wasn't with her, or the van: it was with her wheelchair. For some time now, the right wheel had not pointed in the same direction as the left wheel. Which meant that Amy sometimes felt like she was trying to get around in a supermarket trolley. And not just any trolley: one that's been separated from all the others on the edge of the supermarket car park because, as soon as any shopper sees it, they know that its wheels will stick.

I've maybe gone a bit far with the trolley comparison. Although it was a comparison Amy herself would use a lot while complaining to her mum about her wheelchair. She was doing exactly that when this story begins, as they drove into Lodlil, the cheaper-than-most superstore near where they lived.

Chapter 1

"This story begins

"That one," said Amy, pointing out of the window. "Mum. The rusty one. With the soggy newspaper in it. And the wonky front wheel. *That's* the kind of trolley my wheelchair is like."

"Yes," said Suzi, carefully backing into a space between two cars, into one of which a family was loading a huge amount of shopping. This was hard to do, as the van was large and high in the back, and Amy and her chair were in the way.

More in the way than usual, in fact, as Amy was pointing, with both arms, at the rusty trolley. "Can you see it?"

"No. But I know the one you mean."

"You do?"

"Well. I know the *kind* of one you mean. Because you've pointed one *like* that out every time we've come to the supermarket this month."

"Because, Mum," said Amy, "my wheels have been that wonky for a month!"

Suzi sighed, and switched the van engine off. *Life is as perfect as you want it to be*, she thought to herself. Amy's mum was very keen on "inspirational quotes": positive things people have said about life that you can find all over the internet, normally backed by an image of a sunset. She repeated these to herself in times of stress. Often, though – like now, as she watched the man from the car next to her trying again and again to slam the boot down over a stuck bag containing mainly eggs – they didn't seem to have much effect.

Suzi got out of the driving seat, went round the back of the van, opened the back doors (on which Amy had stuck an ironic **"HOT ROD"** sticker that she'd got from a car magazine called *Fast Wheels*) and pressed a button.

The ramp folded out for Amy to wheel down. Amy turned the chair round to face her mum. But then she carried on turning it, away from her, in a circle. And then another circle. And then another (when she wanted to, Amy could turn her chair very, very fast).

"I can't stop it, Mum!" she called out. "The wheels are doing it by themselves. Help me! Help me! Help me!"

Suzi watched her, with an eyebrow raised. She wondered about just letting her daughter get very, very dizzy and sick. But eventually, after six turns, and no sign of either the pretend screaming stopping or the circling slowing down, she said:

"All right! OK! You win, Amy! I'll talk to your dad. We'll get you a new chair."

Amy stopped and smiled. She reached into her pocket and took out a piece of paper, on which was printed a picture from the internet.

"Thanks, Mum!" she said excitedly. "Here's the one I want!"

Chapter 2
Not a car

"It's brilliant!" said Amy, going up the ramp into the van a few days later.

"I'm glad you like it," said Suzi.

"I love it!" said Amy.

"Great. You can write a letter to your dad, thanking him maybe."

"I already have! I sent him an email telling him how amazing it is. Look!" Amy turned the wheelchair all the way round, inside the van, and came back down the ramp. "It's like a dodgem car!"

She came off the ramp and turned round again, twisting the control lever on her new, black, shiny and, most importantly, *motorised* wheelchair.

Her mum had parked the van in their drive and opened the back doors, so that Amy could practise going up and down the ramp. Which she had been doing for a while.

Quite a long while.

"It's like a dodgem car . . ." echoed Jack, Amy's fourteen-year-old brother, who was standing – or at least slouching, his back against the door – in their front garden, pretending not to be interested.

It was one of the things he did all the time now, repeating back anything that anyone said, in a bored, taking-the-mickey voice. Amy sometimes wondered if, when he was about twelve and a half, her brother had been secretly replaced in the night by a sarcastic echo chamber.

"Well, it is, a bit," said Amy. "Remember when Dad took me on the dodgems, Mum?"

"Of course! He took both of you in one car. You both drove it."

"Yes, but he let me do the steering wheel by myself after a bit. And I swerved through all the other cars. We didn't even bump once!"

"Ha. Yes, that's right! What age were you then?"

"Seven. And then he bought us candyfloss!"

Suzi nodded, and looked down. Amy's dad, Peter, didn't live with them any more. He lived a long way away, in Scotland.

"He said I was a natural driver, didn't he, Mum? *'You're a natural, Amy,'* he said!"

"*You're a natural, Amy . . .*" said Jack. In his bored, taking-the-mickey voice.

"Yes. Unlike his son, who always loses to me when we play *Formula One: Grand Prix!*"

Jack made a rude gesture at her. "*Grand Prix,*" he echoed sarcastically.

"Anyway, Amy . . ." Suzi said, coming out of her little trance, "is that enough practice now?"

"Not quite, Mum . . ." Amy said, turning round

again. "I do love it, but I just want to see if I can do a bit more with it . . . just want to see how it corners . . . how it steers . . . what's its top speed . . ."

"How it corners . . . how it steers . . . what's its top speed . . ."

"Jack, stop doing that," said Suzi. "It's tiresome."

"Well," said Jack, finally speaking in his own voice, which sounded to Amy, as ever, like someone who was convinced he knew *everything*, even though he was only actually two and half years older than her. "Come on. It's a wheelchair. It's not like it's fast or anything."

"It's a Mobilcon XR-207," said Amy. "It uses technology from their go-karts. It has a five-horsepower engine!"

"OK, show me top speed, then," said Jack.

Amy pushed the

lever on the right-hand arm of the chair forward. The chair went down the drive.

Not, it must be said, very fast.

"See?" said Jack. "It's not exactly an Aston Martin DB5, is it?"

This made Amy stop. She looked down.

"I know it's not an Aston Martin DB5," she said quietly.

Suzi frowned. "Oh shush, Jack. If Amy wants to have fun pretending her new wheelchair is like a car, let her."

This did the trick – it shut Jack up. But actually – even though her mum didn't mean it to – it also made Amy feel kind of worse. It made her feel that what she had been doing with her chair in the drive was maybe just that: a babyish game of pretend.

And, at the end of the day, Jack was right: it *wasn't* a car. It was just a wheelchair.

But then Amy had an idea . . .

Chapter 3

The Whiter-Tooth-Whiz 503

"Hmm . . ." said Rahul. "I don't know."

"Come on. You know you can. If anyone can, you can."

Rahul scratched his head, and took his glasses off. This was something he did a lot when he wanted to look closely at something. It made Amy wonder what the point exactly of him having glasses was.

"What is the point of you having glasses?" she

said (because when Amy had a thought, usually she couldn't stop herself from saying it). "When you always take them off anyway to have look at—"

"Shhh," said Rahul. "I'm thinking."

He bent down and stared closely at Amy's new wheelchair. It was, Rahul thought, stylish. It was black and shiny and the wheels were silver and looked like they came from quite a cool bike.

"What's it called?" he said. "This wheelchair?"

"The Mobilcon XR-207."

"Mobilcon!" said Rahul. "They make the coolest stuff. I wanted one of their amazing drones for my birthday, but my parents said it was too expensive. Your chair must have cost a fortune!"

"Yeah . . ." said Amy. "My dad helped pay for it."

Rahul nodded. "It's pretty slick," he said. "XR-207, did you say?"

"Yes," said Amy. "But I prefer to call it . . ."

Amy pulled the lever on the arm of the chair

backwards, and the wheelchair went back, faster than you might think.

". . . The Taylor TurboChaser!"

"Hey!" said Rahul, chasing after her. They were in the playground of their school, Bracket Wood. Amy and Rahul were in Year Six. Amy was the only kid in a wheelchair at the school. The teachers sometimes tried to make her feel OK about this. Which wasn't necessary, as she felt OK about it already.

Her form teacher, Mr Barrington, had once said to her, with an awkward smile on his face, "The way to think about being in a wheelchair, Amy, is that it makes you very special."

And she had told him to bog off. Which she didn't get punished for. Probably because she was in a wheelchair. So in a way, Amy thought later, he was right.

Rahul caught up with her. She pulled the lever to the right – the chair moved smoothly off in that direction. Rahul went towards her, but with a smile she jerked the lever to the left, and the chair went left, dodging him. She stopped and looked up.

"You see? The steering's already as sharp as a Ferrari."

"Yes, OK," he said, breathing heavily. "But there's a long way between that, and me making it into an actual—"

"Rahul!"

He looked over. Their friend Janet was approaching, holding something that looked like a motorcycle helmet, with a toothbrush in the middle of it. Which is exactly what it was.

It was, in fact, an old motorcycle helmet, with a little battery-powered motor at the side, attached to a small metal rod. That rod was then glued to a toothbrush, positioned round about where the mouth of the helmet-wearer would be.

"Yeah?" said Rahul

"This new invention of yours . . ."

"The Whiter-Tooth-Whiz 503. Yes?"

"Is that what it's called?" said Amy.

"Yep."

"So are there . . . like . . . 502 other models?"

Rahul thought about this for a second. "No," he said. "Are there 206 other versions of your wheelchair, the Mobilcon XR-207?"

"I don't think so. Fair point."

"Anyway," said Janet, "it doesn't work."

Rahul frowned and took the Whiter-Tooth-Whiz 503 out of Janet's hands. He pressed a switch on the motor. The rod vibrated: as did the toothbrush.

"Yes, it does work," he said, looking up.

"No," said Janet, who had started looking at her phone. "You said it would clean my teeth. Without me having to do anything. But that's wrong. Because I still have to a) put toothpaste on the brush, and b) move my mouth around so that the brush gets to different teeth."

When Janet said these two points – a) and b) –

she didn't do what people normally do. She didn't hold up two fingers, one at a time, or point to two fingers, or anything.

She just said it. This was because Janet was one of the laziest people who ever lived, and preferred, whenever possible, not to do anything except look at her phone.

Which, in fact, was why she had been very keen on the idea of the Whiter-Tooth-Whiz 503.

"It doesn't work!" said Janet.

"It does!" said Rahul.

"It's meant to be an effort-saving device."

"Yes. To save you *some* of the effort of cleaning your teeth. Not *all* of the effort!"

"I wanted to be able to clean my teeth and text at the same time!"

Rahul sighed.

"You're just lazy," said Janet, which was ironic.

"No, he's not," said Amy. "And he's going to make

this wheelchair into something *incredible*, aren't you, Rahul?"

Rahul swallowed. "Well . . . I'll try," he said.

Which was good enough for Amy.

Chapter 4

"Fun"!

Amy was right: Rahul really was far from lazy.

The Whiter-Tooth-Whiz 503 was only the latest of his inventions. It had been commissioned by Janet. By commissioned, I mean Janet had said, one day, "I hate cleaning my teeth every night, it's so boring," and Rahul had said, "I've got an idea," and gone off, designed and made the machine, brought it back to school, and asked Janet to pay the costs of making it – eight pounds – which, so far, Janet had not paid.

He had also invented:

The **Alarm Clock-to-Dreams Device 4446**. (You may have noticed by now that all Rahul's inventions have random numbers, to make them seem more like proper inventions. This was why he was so interested in the name of Amy's wheelchair.) The Alarm Clock-to-Dreams Device 4446 was an alarm clock fitted with a recording microphone, so that when it woke you up, before it had a chance to vanish into your head, you could shout out what happened in last-night's dream. Rahul was working on an upgrade of this invention, whereby the words would become animated pictures, immediately uploadable to YouTube.

M CLOCK-TO-DREAMS (Device 4446)

Alarm Bells

mic

12
3
9
6

fig 1

clock

Rahul

The **Toast-Butterer 678X.** (Rahul realised while designing this that to sound *really* like a proper invention, he needed to add letters AND numbers.) This was a knife attached to a toaster, which, when the toast popped up, would automatically start buttering it. This did require quite a powerful spring, because if the toast was only halfway out of its slot, the buttering would only butter the top half. Which was not only not as nice, it could also mean the butter would drip down into the toaster and make it explode. As a result of this happening the first time Rahul tried it, the Toast-Butterer 678X had been banned from Rahul's parents' kitchen.

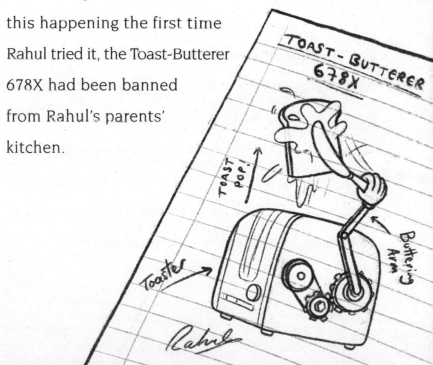

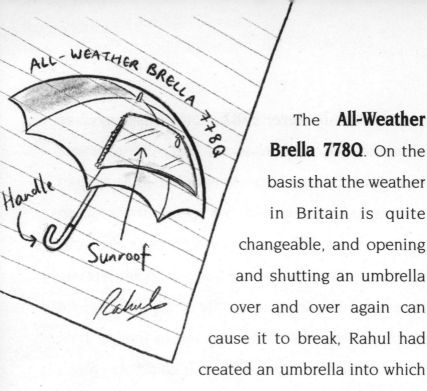

ALL-WEATHER BRELLA 778Q

Handle

Sunroof

Rahul

The **All-Weather Brella 778Q**. On the basis that the weather in Britain is quite changeable, and opening and shutting an umbrella over and over again can cause it to break, Rahul had created an umbrella into which he had built a sun roof (a polythene window with a zip, basically).

The **Snowman Life-Extender XJ59P**. "Have you built a snowman that you're really proud of? That you've spent ages on, and looked out of the window at after a hard and freezing morning's building? Only for it to melt really quickly and depressingly into sludge? Well, worry no more! Because with the Snowman Life-Extender (bespoke-designed to fit your snowman, cooled to -3 degrees) you can keep your favourite snow guy alive for as long as you like (electricity bill permitting). Maybe he might even come alive and fly with you at Christmas to the North Pole! (Disclaimer: no guarantee this will happen.)"

This is a direct quote from the press release that Rahul had written for the Snowman Life-Extender XJ59P. To be honest, he had written the press release for this one before creating the invention itself. But the invention, he always insisted, was on the way.

SNOWMAN LIFE - EXTENDER
XJ59P
Large Snowglobe
Top Hat
Carrot
Thermometer
Snow-man
Freezer Compartment
Plug into mains
Rahul

The **Coffee-Cube-Maker 7777T**. This was a box with a funnel at the top, into which you poured instant coffee, and which would then – at the bottom – spit out the coffee as cubes. "What's the point of that?" said Rahul's father, Sanjay. This was generally not a question that Sanjay asked. Sanjay was 99 per cent convinced that his son was one day going to invent something incredible, and that the whole family would be rich. Thus, he funded Rahul's inventions, and let him plunder the family business – a big retail warehouse called Agarwal Supplies, which stocked all kinds of stuff – for raw materials. But this one

Coffee Cube
Maker 7777T

Coffee in!

funnel

Rahul

Cubes out!

seemed to test him.

"To have coffee as cubes," said Rahul.

"Yes, I see that," said Sanjay. "But when you put them in hot water . . . ?"

"They dissolve."

Sanjay frowned. "Like instant coffee always does."

"Yes," said Rahul. "But they'll look cool in the tin."

Sanjay shrugged and nodded, and put this observation down as one of the many that meant his son was a genius he would never understand.

Bean Pants. This was the only invention that Rahul had made that didn't have a number, because Rahul felt that it went against its brand, which was – and he often said this doing an inverted commas mime – "fun". It was pants, the lining of which he'd filled with beans. Not baked beans: whatever the beans are that are in bean bags. Which meant that, wherever you sat, you could feel like you were sitting on a bean bag.

"Fun"!There were many other inventions on Rahul's slate, by which I mean in his head, or doodles in his rough book.

But these were the biggies. Or at least they were until Amy's wheelchair came along.

Chapter 5

NEEEEWOOOOOWWWW

Rahul sighed, and handed the Whiter-Tooth-Whiz 503 back to Janet.

"Eight pounds, please," he said.

Janet shook her head, and opened her mouth to continue to protest.

But Amy cut her off.

"Hello? Never mind the Whiter-Tooth-Whiz!"

"503."

"What?"

"The Whiter-Tooth-Whiz 503," said Rahul.

"Whatevs." Amy spread out her hands. "*This* is going to be your best invention ever!"

Janet frowned at her. "Rahul's going to invent you?"

"Not me, idiot," said Amy, pointing downwards. "This. The wheelchair."

"Huh? But it's invented already . . ." said Janet. "I can see it very clearly."

"Amy thinks I can *re*-invent it . . ." said Rahul.

"What does that mean?"

"It means . . ." said Amy, "he's going to make it into . . . well, I'll show you."

She turned and faced away from them, towards a free section of the playground, where no other kid was fighting, running or skipping.

"Taylor lines up her car, in pole position on the Indianapolis 500 track."

"Who are you talking to?" said Janet. "And why

has your voice gone so deep?"

"She's being a motor racing commentator, Janet," whispered Rahul.

"Oh," said Janet.

Amy's eyes went up. "She's watching for the chequered flag. A lot of work has gone into this machine since the last race. Rahul, head of her team of mechanics, has turbo-charged its engines, and reworked the tyres, and streamlined the body, and now it's a speed-machine."

She mimed turning a key.

"*Brrrrrrrmmmmmm. Brrrrrrrrrrmmmmm. Brrrrrrrrrrrrrmmmmmmm!* Listen to that! Even from the commentary box we can hear it. It sounds . . ." and here her voice went very deep, as she did an impression of one of the men on a TV show about cars that seemed to always be on some channel somewhere ". . . *like the devil clearing his throat*."

"Right," said Rahul. "I'm really not sure – even

though I am, obviously, great at inventing – that I can make your wheelchair into the kind of vehicle you're imagi—"

"NEEEEEWOOOOOWWWW!" Amy shouted, leaning over to the right, and miming holding a steering wheel (and doing a race-car-speeding-past noise, in case you were wondering).

"NEEEEEEWOOOOWWWWWW!" she shouted again, leaning to the left. "AWAY SHE FLIES!"

Then she sat up, pressed the lever forward, and the chair went off.

At about two miles an hour.

Chapter 6

Easier than the Hulk

"What's going on?" said Suzi.

"What?"

They had once again driven into Lodlil, and once again Suzi had parked with difficulty, opened up the back doors of the van and pressed the button to fold down the ramp.

But then she held up a hand to stop Amy wheeling her chair down it.

"What's going on?" she said again.

"Huh?" said Amy.

"Don't play the innocent with me, Ames. Where's your new chair?"

Amy looked down as if surprised, as if somehow she'd not noticed that she'd come all the way to the supermarket in her old wheelchair. Which, to be fair, her mother hadn't. But then again, Suzi was rushed and tired, and outside their house she had been on the phone arguing with Amy's dad.

"Oh, come on, Amy. Where is it?"

"I'm . . . just getting used to it."

"Pardon?"

"Yes. Um. Turns out that the new wheelchair is a bit . . . fast for me. When you push the lever forward, it moves forward really quick. So . . . I thought I'd leave it in my room for the minute. Until I've got used to it."

Suzi narrowed her eyes at her daughter. "We spent ages on the internet checking out motorised wheelchairs. Specifically: *fastest* motorised wheelchairs. At your request."

"I know but—"

"And your dad – who I've just been on the phone to – paid for most of it. And as Mr 'I'm Not Made of Money', he—"

"Is he still calling himself that?" said Amy.

"Yes, you know how he likes to . . . make himself very clear."

"Wow," said Jack. "You actually spoke to him? Is it Christmas?"

"No, Jack," said Suzi wearily. "It's not Christmas."

"Oh no, that's right. Because if it *was* Christmas, he'd have sent us a depressing card. The one with

Santa Claus in an old car, instead of a sleigh. The same one he's sent us for the last three years."

Jack was speaking

from the passenger seat, without looking up from his phone, or taking off his headphones.

"I love that card!" said Amy, wheeling herself down the ramp. "Shut up, Jack."

"Well, good," said Suzi. "But meanwhile, your new chair wasn't cheap. And if he knows you're not using it – well – he won't be happy."

"Really?"

"You know your dad, Amy. He's not . . . an easy man."

"Oh, I dunno," said Jack. "He's easier than, say, the Hulk. Just."

"OK," said Amy, who hated it when the family conversation began to get a bit anti-Dad, which it did quite a lot. "I'll start using it soon, Mum, don't worry!"

"She's paid someone to pimp her ride, I reckon," said Jack, finally stretching his long legs out of the car. He was at that teenage-boy age where he still looked young, but had grown very tall, a bit like a stretched-out toddler.

"Is that a joke? What does it even mean?" said Suzi.

"It means to make a car all flash and exciting with add-ons and lights and stereo systems and stuff," said Amy. "And of course it's a joke. *Everything* he says is a joke."

"*Everything he says is a joke,*" Jack repeated.

"Well, it is!" said Amy. "Particularly in this case. I mean, it's obvious – one ride you could never pimp is a wheelchair!"

And she wheeled off in her old chair as fast as she could go.

Chapter 7

Better than ALL my other inventions

"**C**ome on . . ." hissed Amy.

"Nearly done!" It was Rahul's voice, calling from inside his workshop. By "workshop", what I mean is his dad's garage, which was at the back of their warehouse. Which they also lived above.

From behind the door came the sound of banging and hammering and scraping. From Amy's point of view, *more* banging and hammering and scraping – she had been outside for nearly an hour.

"Can't I just come in?"

"No!"

"I won't look."

"I don't believe you."

"Hello, Amy!" said Rahul's dad, Sanjay, coming out of the warehouse, a clipboard in hand. "What's happening?"

"I'm making something, Dad!" shouted Rahul.

"Oh good," said Sanjay. "Rahul is a very good inventor, you know, Amy."

"Yes, I know," said Amy.

"One day he's going to invent something incredible. And it's going to make us very rich. I'm one hundred per cent convinced of it."

"Oh! You've gone up a per cent."

"I have?"

"Yes. You normally say ninety-nine per cent."

"Ha! You see, my confidence has gone up! What are you working on, Rahul? Is it the Learning-Toast XF514 . . . ?"

"Is that like the Toast-Butterer 678X . . . ?" said Amy.

"No!" shouted Rahul. "It's a piece of toast that you get from the Toast-Butterer, already well buttered. Then you place it on the book or whatever it is you want to learn from. Then when all the words have soaked into the toast . . . you eat it!"

"What?"

"Yes! And then you learn the words!"

"Brilliant. Quite brilliant!" said Sanjay.

"Right . . ." said Amy.

"And anyway, I'm not working on it."

"The Robotic Returning-Cup Z45?" said his dad. "I love that one."

"Let me guess, Rahul," said Amy. "A cup that flies

back to the sink after you've finished your drink? So your mum doesn't have to pick up lots of cups from your room?"

"Yes! Well, it doesn't fly back, it walks back."

"Walks . . . ?"

"It's got little legs that come out automatically when your cup's empty. Well, it will, when I've finished it. But no, Dad!" he said, raising his voice again. "I'm not working on that either!"

"Oh. What *are* you working on?" said Sanjay. "Something better than all those?"

"Better than ALL my other inventions . . ."

And with that, Rahul pressed the button to open the garage door.

With a metallic groan, it began to rise.

Chapter 8

Upside-down fish tanks

Unfortunately, Rahul's big reveal didn't work that well, as the door creaked and stuttered and, halfway up, got stuck.

"Have you thought about inventing something to make the garage door open easily, Rahul?"

"No, Dad. You need to get that fixed by a grown-up."

"OK. Try pressing the button again."

Rahul did. The door creaked and stuttered again,

but then jerked up, opening all the way —

— to reveal Rahul standing by something.

Actually, it wasn't quite recognisable as *anything* at first.

Somewhere in there — definitely — was Amy's wheelchair. But it was hard to see, as three more chairs had been fastened to it (not wheelchairs — ordinary chairs: one next to Amy's chair, and two behind it).

There was a series of pipes and wires connecting all the bits of it together. And over the whole thing — to make a roof and glass windows — had been placed what looked like two enormous upside-down fish tanks.

"The Taylor TurboChaser . . ." said Rahul proudly, gesturing to it with a big arm movement. Amy and Rahul's dad looked on, open-mouthed. ". . . ZX115," Rahul added.

"You really must get on with the Robotic Returning-Cup," said Sanjay eventually.

Chapter 9

Do you want to go faster?

"Don't you like it?" said Rahul. "I got all the stuff from the disused bits of the warehouse. I mean, it's not finished. I want to add loads more things."

"Um . . ." said Amy.

"That means no," said Rahul, looking sad.

"No. I mean, it doesn't," said Amy, wheeling herself into the garage. "It's amazing. But I thought you'd just be . . . making my wheelchair . . . more flash."

"It *is* a bit more flash."

"Yes, but I mean, I thought you'd do: some lights . . . maybe painting it silver . . . boost the engine a bit . . . a few accessories . . . I didn't think you were *actually* gonna make it into a . . ."

"Car."

"Yes . . ." said Amy. She wheeled slowly, all the way round it. Then she turned to her friend, shook her head and laughed. "Well . . . all I can say is thank you!"

"Don't say that," said Rahul.

"Why not?"

Rahul smiled. "Because you haven't driven it yet . . . !"

It took a little while to get Amy into the driver's seat of the Taylor TurboChaser – Rahul, with a lot of difficulty, had to hold up one of the fish tanks, and Amy had to crawl out of her old chair and lift herself into her new one – but her arms were strong from so much wheeling, and eventually she got there.

Rahul sat in the seat next to her – the passenger seat – and then brought the roof down again. They sat side by side, looking out through the garage door, where there was a tarmac drive leading up to Agarwal Supplies. On one side of the drive sat a full skip with a fridge standing next to it; on the other, six or seven dustbins.

Amy looked down at the direction lever – still there, still part of her original wheelchair.

"So . . . do I just press the lever forward as normal?" said Amy.

"Wait a minute . . ." said Rahul, who was rummaging around in a box underneath his seat. "I have a few add-ons yet."

He sat up, holding a steering wheel. He leant across Amy and attached it to a metal bar in front of her.

"Wow . . . is that from . . ." she began.

"An Xbox, yes. But it'll work. And here on the dashboard I've added some buttons . . ."

Amy looked down. There was a series of switches with pictures on them: one looked a bit like a motorbike, another like a teepee. She shook her head, assuming she would work out what they were when she needed them (which, to let you in on a secret, is also what all grown-ups do when they see buttons with strange designs on them in cars).

"Will the engine be powerful enough to drive it with all this extra weight on it?" Amy said.

Rahul smiled. "I souped up the engine."

"You put soup into the engine? Chicken, veg or tomato?"

Rahul frowned. "No, it's a . . . thing . . . that people say . . . when they mean made it more powerful . . ."

Now Amy smiled. "I know that, Rahul. I subscribe to three different motoring magazines."

"Oh, sorry. It was a joke, wasn't it? I'm not very good with jokes."

Amy shook her head, and then gripped the lever.

"Just one more thing," said Rahul, reaching across her and fitting her with the seat belt.

"You made these too?" said Amy, as he clicked himself in after her.

"Well, kind of. If you consider using my trusty screwdriver to get them out of my parents' car to be 'making'."

"Er . . . won't they, sort of, *miss* those?"

"Don't worry. My parents hardly ever use the car,"
said Rahul. "And anyway, I'll put them back. At some
point."

Amy smiled to herself. She wanted to say: *We
won't really need those, will we? I mean it's not going to
go that fast. And I'm never going to be driving it that far.*
But she thought that might upset her friend, and
Amy was a *good* friend. So she just pushed the lever
forward. The Taylor TurboChaser moved. Quite
slowly. In fact, quite a lot *more* slowly than it had
before. A minute later, they were still in the garage.

"Um . . ." said Amy.

"Oh," said Rahul, "do you want to go faster?"

"A bit, yes."

"Try pushing the lever forward a bit more. I've
adjusted it so it works like an accelerator pedal now,
so you can control the speed properly."

Amy looked down at her hand on the lever.

"It's pushed all the way forward," she said.

Rahul looked at the position of the lever too. He nodded slowly.

"OK . . ." he said. He pulled open a little door in the dashboard.

"What's that?" said Amy, looking inside. There was a small box in there with a red button in it.

"It's the turbo part of the TurboChaser. This button pushes power to the engine, and speeds everything up ten times!"

"Oh great!" Amy said, pressing it. And immediately the vehicle shot forward like a rocket.

"AAAAARGGH!" screamed Amy.

"AAAAARGGH!" screamed Rahul. "Stop! Stop!"

"I don't know where the brakes are!" screamed Amy.

Chapter 10

Who taught you to do that?

"**P**ress the—" began Rahul.

But it was too late!

They were heading directly for the corrugated-iron doors of Agarwal Supplies, and Amy didn't have time to look down at her fingers. The only time she had was what you might call "reflex time" – that is, the split second when the body takes over and does something by instinct.

And the thing that Amy's body suddenly found

itself able to do, despite never having really done it before, was *drive*.

Amy gripped the steering wheel with both hands and jerked it all the way round to the left. The Taylor TurboChaser, with surprising smoothness, followed, curving away from the warehouse doors and out into the industrial estate.

But now they were heading right for the skip!

So again, instinct kicked in, and Amy lurched the wheel back to the right, just missing the fridge that had been dumped next to the skip.

Which would
have meant they
were through this
sudden and unexpected
obstacle race, had it not
been for . . . the dustbins!

"AAARGH!"

The dustbins were arranged in a
way that avoiding them completely was
almost impossible. Turning away from
one would have meant driving straight at
another. Amy's only choice was to slalom! Which,
for those of you who have never seen someone
skiing, means "zigzag"!

So she did, turning the wheel very quickly this way and that, making the vehicle rock on its sides as it twisted and turned past one dustbin, then another, then another, then all of them.

She brought the TurboChaser back round. It was still powering away from the dustbins.

"—blue button!" finished Rahul.

"What?"

"I'm finishing my sentence from about three minutes ago! Press the blue button! It's a brake!"

"Oh!" said Amy, and she pressed it.

The Taylor TurboChaser came to an abrupt halt: a very abrupt halt – Amy and Rahul were thrown forward in their seats in a way that made Amy very thankful indeed for the seat belts.

"Wow!" said Rahul, as gravity settled him back into his seat. "Who taught you to do that?"

"No one," said Amy. "I just did what came naturally!"

"Well, you can really drive!"

Amy looked at him. "I guess I can. And you, my friend, can really invent. Because what you've made here – " she said, holding her arms up and taking in the whole vehicle " – is a supercar!"

Chapter 11

A dip in her stomach

"Hi, Dad!"

"Amy . . . how are you?"

"I'm fine, Dad. How are you?"

"Oh, not bad. I've got a lot of work on. But you don't want to know about that."

Actually, Dad, Amy wanted to shout down the phone, *I DO want to know about that.* She was sitting in their hallway, speaking to her dad on the landline (she wasn't allowed a phone yet, which was annoying, as Jack was on his ALL the time).

Peter Taylor, her dad, called about once a week, and Amy really looked forward to it, even if sometimes she looked back afterwards on their conversations as not being quite what she had hoped for. Jack wouldn't speak to their dad at all.

But, yes, Amy did want to know about her dad's job, because her dad's job was . . . designing cars! Supercars – which are basically very fast cars – to be exact. Some of them even had his name – and therefore *her* name – on them!

"Are you working on the new GT 500, Dad, or is it—" she began.

"What? Oh yes. The meeting. Of course. Just give me two minutes." Amy realised he was speaking to someone else on the other end. But then his voice became loud again. "What were you saying, Amy?"

And then before she could answer he said, "How's the new chair?"

"Oh yes, it's great! Thank you so much!"

"No need to thank me. Although you could send me a photo of you in it. That would be nice."

"Er . . . yes. At some point."

"Pardon, Amy?" He spoke suddenly strictly, which he sometimes did.

"Sorry, Dad, yes. I will. Soon."

"OK. Can I speak to your mum?"

Amy felt a dip in her stomach. So often when she talked to her dad, the conversation ended sooner than she would like.

"Sure, Dad. *Mum!*"

"And, Amy?" he said.

"Yes?"

"I'd really like to see you in that chair. Mobilcon's prices are daylight robbery – I'd like to know it's worth it."

Amy nodded. Which was pointless, because he couldn't see.

And gulped.

Which he couldn't see either.

Chapter 12

Dank meme

Later that day, the Taylors went out for a walk. This was always difficult. Not because Amy was in a wheelchair. But because of Jack.

"Come on, Jack!" shouted Suzi, as she and Amy waited at the door. "How many times do I have to tell you?"

"*How many times do I have to tell you?*" came back from inside the house, in a stupid voice.

Suzi and Amy exchanged glances.

"Your sister can't walk!" shouted Suzi. "And *she's* coming out for a walk!"

"Yeet!" said Jack, shambling out of his room. "Walking is for Normies. It's a dank meme."

"Please speak English."

"He doesn't want to come," said Amy.

"He doesn't want to come."

"That means you have to come now," said Amy. "If you're being sarcastic about not wanting to come, it means you want to come."

Jack looked a bit confused. But then said, "OK!" and put his shoes on.

It turned out that there *was* an Amy-centred problem with the walk, though.

"Amy! *Where* is your new chair?" said Suzi. "I'm fed up with watching you struggling with that old one!"

"I told you, Mum. I'm still getting used to it. I just want to use it on small journeys."

"This *is* a small journey. It's a walk round the

park. But it's taking a long time. Because you're going round and round in circles. Because that old wheelchair's stuck wheel has got even worse."

Amy – who was indeed completing a circle rather than going forward – stopped and sighed.

"Amy," said her mum. "Please. I've been to your room. It's not there. So . . . where *is* your new—"

"OK, OK. I'll show you. This way!" said Amy, moving off. Or trying to, at least.

"Sorry, which way?" said Jack, after a few seconds of the wheelchair turning round and round.

"Yeah, yeah, point taken," said Amy. "Can you help turn me round, please? And then just push me for a bit?"

Chapter 13

Click!

"OK, Mum," said Amy, as she sat in her old chair outside Rahul's dad's garage. "You remember that inspirational quote you like to tell me . . ."

"Which one?" said Suzi.

"The one about 'Don't dream dreams: make them come true'."

"Oh yes, I like that one."

"Well . . ." said Amy, "I . . . with Rahul's help . . . have kind of done that."

Suzi nodded. "OK. Well. Good!" But then frowned. "How do you mean?"

Amy looked towards the garage and then back at her mum.

"You *promise* you won't get upset?" she said.

"Er . . . that's never a good thing when anyone says that, Amy. How can I promise I won't get upset, without knowing what I'm about to see?"

"No. I get that. But I'd like you to say it anyway."

"What, meaninglessly?"

"Yes," said Amy.

Suzi sighed. "Right. I promise I won't get upset."

Rahul, who was standing by the side of the garage with a new remote control, pressed the button. The door came up halfway towards Amy, Suzi and Jack. Then stopped.

"Rahul! I thought you said you were going to get a grown-up to fix the garage door?" said Amy.

"I was. But my dad wasn't bothered."

"I wasn't bothered!" shouted Sanjay from somewhere in the warehouse.

"He said as long as it opens eventually, what's the rush?"

"What's the rush?" Sanjay shouted again.

"So you made that remote control?" said Amy.

"I did," said Rahul, pressing the button again. The door shook, but didn't move.

"Hmm. I'm starting to worry about your inventing capabilities."

"NOT AS MUCH AS I AM!"

They looked round. It was Suzi who had shouted. It was definitely her, even though they could only see her bottom half, under the garage door. Which she'd crept under while they were talking.

"I think your mum might have found the Taylor TurboChaser . . ." said Rahul.

"Yes," said Amy. "I think she might."

"HA HA HA HA HA HA HA HA HA HA!"

"I think your brother might have found it too."

Amy wheeled herself under the door, followed by Rahul. When they were both inside the garage, they waited, for about a minute, for Suzi to turn round.

Suzi, though, was just staring and staring at what had become of Amy's new wheelchair. It seemed for so long that Amy began to hope that perhaps her mum had started to like it.

Eventually Amy said, hopefully: "It's called the Taylor TurboChaser . . . ZX115."

This, finally, made Suzi turn round.

Her face was looking very pale.

There was a long pause.

"WHAT ARE YOU THINKING OF AMY WHAT HAVE YOU DONE WHAT EVEN IS IT NOW IT DOESN'T EVEN LOOK LIKE A WHEELCHAIR IT JUST LOOKS MAD WHAT AM I GOING

TO TELL YOUR FATHER OH MY LORD AMY YOU ARE THE END OF THE WORLD!"

"Mum," said Amy, realising that, no, her mum hadn't started to like it, "you promised you wouldn't get upset."

"MEANINGLESSLY!"

"It's great, Mum! It goes really fast!"

"It does, Mrs Taylor!" said Rahul. "It's like a wheelchair supercar!"

"Oh, fantastic. Thanks, Rahul. Really. Not only have you made Amy's new wheelchair look like a mad thing from . . . from . . ."

"Mario Kart," said Jack, very seriously (the only thing he didn't joke about was video games).

"*Mario Kart?*" said Rahul. "I think it's much more like

something from Grand Theft Auto."

"Mario Kart," said Jack firmly. "Be glad I didn't say Yoshi."

"I think there is a bit of an element of Mater, the truck from *Cars*," said Sanjay, who had bent himself under the door to see what all these people were doing in his garage.

"That's what I think Mum's van looks like," said Amy.

"Anyway, that *is* actually a video game as well as a movie," said Jack.

"HELLO?" said Suzi. "CAN WE STOP TALKING ABOUT WHAT VIDEO-GAME CAR IT LOOKS LIKE?"

"Well, you were the one trying to think of something," said Amy.

"YES! BECAUSE THERE'S NEVER BEEN ANY WHEELCHAIR THAT'S EVER LOOKED LIKE THAT! BUT NOW YOU TELL ME IT

GOES REALLY FAST AS WELL? SO YOU'RE GOING TO KILL YOURSELF IN A CROSS BETWEEN A DUMP TRUCK, A SOFA AND AN AQUARIUM?"

Everyone looked at the Taylor TurboChaser.

"Good shout," said Sanjay. "That pretty much sums it up."

"It's my dream, Mum . . ." said Amy, her voice wobbling ever so slightly. "I'm trying to make it come true."

Suzi looked at her. Her face – and voice – softened.

"Oh, Amy. I understand that. But—"

Click!

"What was that?" said Amy. They all turned round. Jack was standing a little way away, having clearly just taken a photo of the vehicle with his phone. Which he was holding out. Then he looked down at his screen and started tapping.

"Jack!" said Amy. "Don't put it on Instagram!"

"I'm not!" said Jack.

"Oh, OK."

"I've put it on my Snapchat Stories."

"Oh no!" said Amy.

"What's the problem?"

"Dad checks your Snapchat!" she screamed.

"He *does*?" said Jack.

Chapter 14

Quite a pill

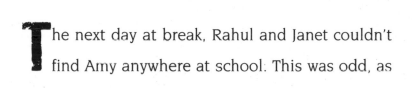

The next day at break, Rahul and Janet couldn't find Amy anywhere at school. This was odd, as she had definitely been in class for the register.

"Has she gone home, maybe?" said Janet to Rahul. They were walking together down one of the school corridors, looking around.

"I don't think so. Her mum would've had to come and get her, and she works quite a long way away, I think."

Then suddenly they heard a noise, small but unmistakable – a sob. They looked round, and saw that they were passing the school's one disabled toilet.

Rahul and Janet exchanged glances.

"Amy . . . ?" said Rahul nervously. "Are you in there?"

"Yes . . ." came a quiet voice back.

"What's it like?" said Janet.

There was a pause. Rahul looked at her and frowned.

"Pardon?" said Amy.

"Well," said Janet, "you know that the standard toilets in this place are terrible. I just wondered if yours was maybe a bit nicer? I know it's definitely bigger than any of ours."

"OMG, Janet . . ." said Rahul. "Can't you hear she's crying?"

"Yes, Janet," said Amy, "it's like Buckingham

Palace in here. I've got my own TV and personal butler."

"*Really?*" said Janet.

"No," said Amy, opening the door. "But thanks. I *was* crying, and now you've made me laugh."

They went into the playground, where some boys – Barry Bennett and Malcolm Bailey and Alfie Moore and Sam Green and Ryan Ward – were playing football. They were making a lot of noise, which meant that Amy and Janet and Rahul could talk about why Amy had been crying without anyone noticing.

"What happened, Amy?" said Rahul. "Is it something to do with yesterday?"

"Yes," said Amy.

"And the Taylor TurboChaser   ?"

She nodded, but said, "I'm not allowed to call it that any more."

Janet frowned. "Why?"

"Because after we got home, my dad FaceTimed. He had seen the photo on Jack's Snapchat."

"Oh," said Rahul. "Was he cross?"

Amy went quiet. "He doesn't really shout or anything, my dad. He just goes very . . . cold."

"Do his lips go blue?" said Janet.

"No, Janet. I don't mean his *temperature* goes down. I mean he starts speaking very quietly and definitely and slowly . . ." Her lip trembled as she said this. She took a deep breath. "Anyway, he was speaking like that, and he said he was very . . . disappointed in me. And that the new wheelchair cost a lot of money and that we had to take off all the things that you put on it, Rahul . . . and turn it back into an ordinary chair."

"Did you tell him how amazing it is? I thought he loved cars too."

"I tried, but he wouldn't listen. He didn't want to hear about how fast it can go, or how well it can corner, or anything. He just said that what we had done to it was silly and idiotic and dangerous and probably illegal. He said he wanted to see a picture of the wheelchair with all of the extras taken off. By Sunday."

"Sunday?" cried Rahul. "That's in three days!"

"Yes. He's going away then. To Japan, for the start of the Formula One season. He wants it done before that. Or else he's going to send Mobilcon to pick it up."

Rahul went very quiet. Even Janet seemed to understand that this was bad.

"But what wheelchair will you use, then?" said Rahul, looking down.

"My old one, I suppose."

"But one wheel doesn't work!"

"Well. I suppose he thinks it won't come to that. That we'll just convert the TurboChaser back to being a wheelchair. Which . . ." she shrugged her shoulders, "I suppose we will. He's probably right, anyway. It probably *is* illegal and dangerous and—"

"Your dad's quite a pill, isn't he?" interrupted Janet.

"Pardon?"

"It's something my mum says. It doesn't mean that he's a small thing like medicine that you have to swallow."

"Yes, I guessed that."

"It means he's hard work. Like pills can be!"

"Yes, well," said Amy. "He didn't use to be. He was really nice. Once. But then after my accident . . . I don't know . . . that's when he got more . . . cold."

"Is that when he left?" said Janet, who tended to put things bluntly.

"Um," said Amy. "Yes."

Rahul looked up. "I'm so sorry, Amy. It's all my fault. I should never have pimped it."

"I'm not allowed to use that phrase either."

"Oh."

"But it *isn't* your fault. I wanted you to do that. I don't want something that crawls along; I want something that flies!"

"What, in the air?" said Janet.

"I don't know if I can do that," said Rahul.

"No! I mean along the road. I dreamt of it being . . . well, like it is." She lowered her voice to a whisper. "The Taylor TurboChaser."

Rahul nodded and sighed. "I suppose there's nothing we can do. I'll start taking it apart tonight."

"Yes," said Amy. The bell rang for the end of break. Amy started turning her wheelchair round. And then round again. And then again.

Suddenly a stern but kind voice rang out over the playground. "Amy Taylor! Are you intending to join us for the rest of the day?"

Amy turned to see Mr Carter, the head teacher,

standing by the door, holding it open.

"Rahul," she said, "can you . . . um . . . push me back to class, please?"

Rahul started pushing.

"Any time today!" called Mr Carter.

Janet grabbed the other handle of the wheelchair and, together, she and Rahul started running. Someone had left a football on the ground – Amy steered round it!

Then swerved left, past an abandoned jumper!

Then slalomed round a rucksack, a new kid looking lost and a cone that had been left out from a PE lesson!

Which was all quite difficult with a dodgy wheel, but – powered by Rahul and Janet, at least – she managed it.

They screeched through the door and into the corridor.

"Well done!" said Mr Carter, as they slowed down

and he shut the door. "You'll be a racing driver one day, Amy."

Amy looked at him. "No," she said sadly. "Not now, I won't."

Chapter 15

The photo

Back at home, Amy lay on her bed.

All around the room, on the walls, were pictures of cars cut out of magazines: the DB5, the Gullwing, the E-Type, and many others.

Normally, Amy liked to rest her eye on these when she was in her bedroom. But today, her view was blocked by her old wheelchair, which was parked next to her bed. She sighed, knowing she could always look round it – but it felt to her that even if she moved her head, all she would see was the contrast between those cars and her chair, with its still-wonky wheel.

Instead, she looked at one other picture in her room, a framed one by her bed.

She reached over and lifted it closer to her – it was from a family holiday they had taken about five years ago. Her dad had been driving what was then the family car – an old classic called a Bristol, which he'd reconditioned himself – but had suddenly stopped by a lake in the country and insisted everyone got out so he could take a photo. He had set up his camera on a timer so he could be in it too.

Her mum and dad stood in the middle of the picture, their arms round each other. On the right-hand side stood Jack, not making a stupid face or a rude gesture to camera, or anything, and on their left, Amy.

They were all laughing, even Jack. Amy looked

at it now and tried to remember what had been so funny. She shook her head. It had gone. All she could remember was that they all seemed to laugh a lot more in those days.

A tear started to mist up her vision. There was a knock on the door. Amy didn't much like crying, or feeling sorry for herself – and, certainly, she didn't like to be *seen* crying, or feeling sorry for herself – so she wiped it away.

Her mum came in.

"Are you all right, love?"

Suzi came and sat on the edge of Amy's bed.

"Yes, Mum," Amy said. "It's fine. Whatever."

Suzi, like any mum, knew that the words "it's fine" and "whatever", when said by her child, always meant the opposite.

"Amy . . ." she said, "I know you really loved what Rahul did to your wheelchair, the . . . Kerb-O-Blaster . . ."

"TurboChaser!" said Amy.

"Right."

"It wasn't just what Rahul did to it, Mum." Amy looked at her car posters. "It was . . . *driving* the TurboChaser. It was the *best*, Mum. It felt nearly . . . nearly like flying. Or something."

Suzi nodded.

"I thought maybe . . ." Amy continued, "somehow . . . I could end up racing it. Somewhere." She shrugged. "Stupid idea, I know. And now I never will, anyway."

Suzi smiled. She pointed at the only poster in the room that wasn't of a car. Which they had put up after the accident, during Amy's long physio sessions.

"What does that poster say, Amy?" she said.

"You know what it says. It's one of your inspirational quotes. It's got a sunset behind it."

"Tell me."

"*Believe in yourself,*" Amy said wearily, "*and the rest will fall into place.*"

"Exactly," said Suzi. "If you believe you're going to drive a car in a race – maybe not the Trouble-Racer . . ."

"TurboChaser!"

"Right. TurboChaser. At some point, you will drive a car in a race. I know you will."

"But how, Mum? How?"

"I dunno . . ." said Suzi, shaking her head. "*Only those who dare to fail greatly achieve greatly. Trust your instincts — they'll never betray you. I get knocked down, but I get up again! If you want to see the big picture, look out for the tiny detail."*

"Those are just more inspirational quotes!"

"Yes. You're right. Apart from the 'I get knocked down' one. I think that's an old pop song."

"So how do they help? What do they even mean?"

"I don't know exactly, darling. All I know is they help me, at least a bit, when things don't feel so good. Now time for sleep. It's Saturday tomorrow! A new day. And *Always think of every new day as a new—"*

"OK, Mum. Enough quotes already."

Suzi nodded.

"Got it."

She kissed her daughter on the forehead and went out. Amy smiled to herself — she knew her mum was trying her best to make her feel better. Even if the quotes sometimes just seemed to be nonsense.

Just before she fell asleep, though, one of them

came back into her head: *If you want to see the big picture, look out for the tiny detail.* Hmm . . . That was kind of a weird one. And it made her think of something – about the photo she had just been looking at before her mum came in.

She reached over, clicked on her bedside light and picked up the photo again. She brought it close to her face. The car door was open, and on the passenger seat was lying . . . a map. The Bristol, being an old car, hadn't had a sat nav. So instead, there was a map, on the seat, which had a route marked out on it in pen, a long arrow running all the way from the south to the north of the country.

A thought came to her, a crazy, mad, wild thought. She rolled off the bed, and on to her chair. Quietly, so as not to disturb her mum, who was in the living room watching telly, she wheeled herself out into the hall, where their phone was, and dialled a number.

"Hello? Rahul?" she said. "You haven't started taking the TurboChaser apart yet, have you? No. Good. Oh, you're about to? Well . . ."

She took a deep breath and said: *"Don't.* I have a plan . . ."

Chapter 16

Let me get this straight

"I can't believe I'm doing this," said Jack, helping his sister put on a dark top to match her dark trousers.

"Shh," said Amy.

"I'm already whispering," he said.

"No, you're not. You don't even know how loud your voice is since it broke. You'll wake Mum up!"

"You'll wake Mum up!"

"Now is not the time to do the repeating thing.

But if you must, do it in a whisper!"

It was midnight. Jack had on black clothes too. He brought her chair – the old one – round to the side of her bed. As he helped her into it, he said, "Shall we leave a note for Mum?"

Amy frowned. "I thought about that. But we'll be there by tomorrow, if everything goes according to plan. Then we can call her, first thing."

Jack nodded, although he looked a bit doubtful. He settled her into her chair, crouched down and looked directly at her.

"OK? You sure you want to do this?"

Amy looked up. She could see his face, lit by the hallway light outside her door. His expression was, she thought, amazingly serious. It had been a long time since she had seen it look like that.

"Yes," she said, "I'm sure."

Amy had always known she would need Jack's help. She needed someone to assist her in getting from her house to Sanjay's garage. Which, even though it was only a few streets away, was not easy – she was, after all, disabled. Plus her wheelchair, the old one that hadn't been made into a supercar, didn't go forward in a straight line, unless someone else was pushing it.

When she'd first approached Jack with her mad, crazy, wild idea, the conversation had gone like this:

"Let me get this straight," Jack had said. "Your plan is to drive *to Scotland*, to show Dad your insane vehicle, and you think he's going to be *pleased*? Oh, and he's leaving for Japan on Sunday and it's currently Friday night."

"Yes," Amy had replied, nodding.

"In that . . . crazy wheelchair thing that Rahul made?"

"The Taylor TurboChaser. Yes."

"Are you on drugs? Have you lost your mind?"

"Probably. I mean, not the first one. The second."

"On the *motorway*?"

"No, I think I lost it somewhere round here."

"Ha ha." This was not a real ha ha. "Good meme." This was not real praise. "You're going to drive that thing – with your friends – on the motorway? For, like, six hundred kilometres?"

"No. Back roads. Late at night. When there's hardly any other cars around."

"Right."

Amy suddenly felt a bit scared. "It's only *just* Scotland. I've checked it on the map. It's only a few miles from the border with England."

"Oh, that makes all the difference."

"I just think if he sees what an amazing thing the TurboChaser is – and that we were able to drive it all that way – he'll change his mind about it," she said. She looked up at her brother. "Won't he?"

Jack made a face – not a particularly encouraging one.

Amy sighed. "Is it a really stupid idea?" she said.

"Amazingly," said Jack. "Bad meme."

There was a short pause when Amy thought, *OK, well, that's that, then.*

Then Jack said, "I'll come to your room at midnight."

Chapter 17

Oh. My. Days.

So that was how Amy managed – still not at all sure why Jack had decided to help her, but happy, because he was good at carrying her, and at pushing her wobbly-wheeled chair – to get to Sanjay's garage at a quarter past midnight on a Friday night.

When they arrived at the industrial estate, they went into the warehouse via the back door, and then through to the garage itself, where, waiting, were

Rahul and . . . was it Janet? Oh yes, thought Amy, with a weary inward sigh, it was.

"Janet!" said Amy. "I told you to wear dark clothes! We're hoping not to be seen!"

"I know. But all my dark clothes were in the wash."

"So you chose to wear . . . a fairy costume?"

Which was indeed what Janet was wearing. A pink satin dress, with a pink crown and glittery wings.

"Yes," said Janet. "I had it left over from a fancy-dress party. I thought it might come in useful."

Amy stared at her. "In what way?"

Janet frowned. "I haven't really worked that out yet."

"OK. Never mind. Rahul, have we got everything we need?"

"I think so. Janet's done the food."

Janet held up a big plastic bag marked LODLIL.

"Hmm," said Amy.

"And for everything else, I've raided a whole load of stuff from the warehouse."

"Won't your dad miss any of it?"

"Well, we can put it all back when we come back. It's all in the car now."

"The car?"

"The TurboChaser, of course."

Amy smiled, excited just at the passing, casual way Rahul had referred to her new wheelchair as a car. Maybe, now, it really was.

"OK," she said. "Did you manage to fit everything in?"

"Oh yeah," said Rahul. "I've carried on working on it. It's got windows now!"

"Windows?"

"Well, cat flaps."

"Pardon?" said Amy.

"I found these cat flaps in the warehouse. I don't think they sold because they're very, very big. Maybe they were designed for lions?"

"Right. Yes. That probably is why they didn't sell. What with no one having one of those for a pet."

"Yes. So anyway, I've cut big rectangles in the fish tanks for them, and you can slide them open for ventilation. And even use them to get in and out of the car. Because also we don't have doors."

"OK . . ." said Amy.

"Right," said Jack, who had been quiet so far. "So where is this *car*?" He landed heavily on the word "car" with all his teenage-boy sarcasm. "Where is the Fart-On Burpo-Your-Facer that's supposedly going to take you all to Scotland?"

"Good meme," said Amy sarcastically.

"It's called the Taylor TurboChaser," said Janet.

"Thanks, Tinkerbell," said Jack. "Anyway. Where is it?"

"It's under here!" said Rahul, who didn't really get sarcasm. He moved towards the centre of the garage, where something stood covered by an enormous black piece of tarpaulin. "I've been keeping it protected; it's a bit damp in here."

And, with something of a flourish, like he was a magician on stage, he pulled off the tarpaulin.

"Oh. My. Days . . ." said Jack.

"And. Mine," said Amy. "You *have* added to it. Wow!"

Chapter 18

So jokes

Rahul beamed proudly.

The machine he was standing next to was now about twice as big as it had been previously. It still had two upside-down fish tanks making up the basic structure, but an old chest, like something out of a pirate ship, had been screwed on the back to make a boot. There were still four chairs, but the three passenger ones now had different-coloured covers: red, green and rainbow. On the front were a series of torches and lanterns, and something that looked a bit like a standard lamp from an office. A tall chimney-like structure stood out on top of the roof.

The car sat squat on four enormous tyres that looked, at least on this vehicle, like they were taken from a monster truck. There were, indeed, four enormous cat flaps cut into the sides of the fish tanks. All over the whole thing there were small

bits and pieces that, frankly, didn't look at all like they belonged there. They certainly didn't look like normal parts of any car Amy had seen before.

And on the front of it was a number plate, on which Rahul had carefully painted TAYTURB1.

"Is Amy's wheelchair even still *in* there?" said Jack.

"Yes!" said Rahul. "Mobilcon really know their onions. The wheelchair is the *heart* of the TurboChaser. I've just . . . . added to it."

"Do they actually make onions as well?" said Janet.

Amy rolled her eyes. "And it . . . still moves?" she said.

"Oh yes," said Rahul. "It's powerful!"

"Oh, hang on," said Amy. "What about its carbon footprint? I forgot to ask about that."

"Neutral! It's electric. Get in, I'll show you some of its new tricks!"

The four of them approached the car. Then stopped.

"How *do* we get in?" said Janet. "Since it doesn't have any doors."

"Good start," said Jack.

"Don't worry," said Rahul. "We just squeeze in through the giant cat flaps. Well, you and I can, Janet – we're small enough."

"And me?" said Jack.

"Well," said Rahul, "Amy said you weren't coming."

"Oh yeah," said Jack. "Course."

"For you, Amy," Rahul continued, "I think we'll have to lift up the right-hand fish tank."

He pointed. One of the upside-down fish tanks had a handle on the side, which looked as if it might normally belong on an old fridge.

"This handle was from an old fridge," said Rahul, grabbing it and straining a bit

"Yes, I thought so," said Amy. "Do you need a hand?"

"No, it's OK. I designed it to be . . ."

"Really difficult?" said Jack, putting his slightly bigger hand on the handle.

The two of them managed to heave it open, and then Rahul, Janet and Amy – with quite a lot of clambering over each other, and Jack having to lift Amy almost above his head to get her into the driving one – got in the seats. Amy was in the front; Rahul in the passenger seat; Janet in the back, with an empty seat next to her – which was good as it gave her room to spread her glittery wings.

Jack stood by, watching.

"So," said Rahul to Amy, "it still drives like it did before. The brakes, by the way – you kind of missed them last time – are here, in the centre of the steering wheel."

"OK. Where's the horn?"

"There," said Rahul, pointing to a can that was hanging down on her right side. Its top half was poking through what appeared to be another cat flap in the roof. She reached up.

"Don't press it. It's an air horn. They make a very loud noise. Plus they work on gas, and it might run out."

"Is that . . . a cat flap in the roof as well?"

"Yes."

"I thought so." She pointed at the "dashboard" – a few bits of wood painted black behind the steering wheel. It had loads of bits and pieces fixed to it. "This clock . . ."

"Yes, it's an alarm clock."

"Isn't it the alarm clock from the Alarm Clock-to-Dreams Device 4446?"

"Yes. I'm suspending production of that for the minute so that we can use it just as the car clock."

"When is your dad leaving for Japan?" said Janet.

"Late on Sunday," said Amy.

"No, but when exactly?"

"Um . . ."

"He's getting a flight at two," said Jack. "So he'll be leaving his work about midday."

"Let's set it for midday on Sunday, then," said Janet. "So that we don't miss it!"

"Can we do that?" said Amy.

"I'll give it a go," said Rahul.

"Hmm," said Jack. "If we *do* miss that time, how will the alarm clock going off help? Won't it just make us feel worse?"

Janet stared at Jack. "I'm glad you're not coming with us."

"What is this little screen?" said Amy, pointing at something else on the dashboard.

"It's a sat nav," said Rahul.

"What, a real one? Not one you've knocked together out of a compass and some bits of string?"

"No. My dad gets some direct from the factory that makes them. He gave me this one to play with a while ago, because there's something wrong with its voice."

"What?"

"You'll see. Also," said Rahul, "we now have lights!"

He clicked on some switches next to the sat nav. The inside of the garage door lit up.

"Wow! Bright. Kind of."

"Bit speckled. But I'll keep improving it . . . plus, on the back, we've got indicators now." He gestured to a series of black felt-tip pens, taped together to form a single stalk next to the steering wheel. Amy pushed it down. Rahul bent forward and from under the chair took out a small pyramid-like object. He opened it up – a little upright pendulum on the front of it went from right to left

"What's that?" said Amy.

"It's called a metronome. Piano players use it to keep time. Listen."

Amy did. Each time the pendulum went backwards and forwards, the metronome went tick. *Tick. Tick. Tick.*

"Have you brought a keyboard?" said Janet, from the back. "Are we going to be singing as we go?"

"No! It's a sound effect. For the indicator. You know, in your mum or dad's car, when they click down on the indicator . . . that's what the sound is . . . *Tick. Tick. Tick.*"

"Wow," said Jack. "You really have thought of everything."

"Thank you," said Rahul, who, as we know, didn't really get sarcasm. "I haven't really worked out a sound system . . . although I have taped this portable wireless speaker to the dashboard . . . but I don't have a phone."

"Your dad's warehouse doesn't have phones?" said Amy.

"Yes, but my dad won't let me have one."

"Does he let you steal most of his stock and drive it to Scotland normally?" said Jack.

"No," said Rahul, confused.

"I've got mine!" said Janet.

"Of course you have," said Amy.

Janet took out a pink sparkly phone. "With its new cover! I chose it specially, to go with this outfit!"

"I think we should be getting on," said Amy. "It's already half past midnight. I was hoping to do most of the journey tonight."

"OK," said Rahul.

"OK," said Janet.

"OK," said Jack, heaving the fish tank up again, and getting into the back of the car next to Janet.

Amy turned round. "What are you doing?"

"Getting into the car. Ow! Get your wing out of my face!"

"Get your face out of my wings!" said Janet.

"You're coming with—?" began Amy.

"Of course I am."

"Why?"

"Well, I could say because I'm your older brother, and *as* your older brother I feel you need someone a bit more mature and responsible around to make sure you make it back in one piece. But the real answer is: this whole trip is going to be just SO JOKES!"

Chapter 19

Like someone torturing a hundred bats

"**O**K," said Amy. "Let's go."

She pushed the direction lever forward.

The Taylor TurboChaser started to move forward. Slowly.

"Oh . . ." said Rahul. "I hadn't bargained for Jack coming. With a fourteen-year-old boy in the car . . ."

"What are you saying, Rahul?" said Jack.

"Well. We're a bit heavier now than I planned. It's going to use more power."

"How *very* dare you," said Jack, with a raised eyebrow.

"It's OK. We've still got this." Rahul pulled open the little door in front of him marked **ONLY IN EMERGENCIES**, containing the turbo button that Amy had pressed the other day. "I was hoping not to use it so early, but . . ."

"What is it?" said Jack, peering at the little switch.

"Turbo," said Amy.

"Cool," said Jack.

"And will it still work?" said Amy. "With the extra weight?"

"I don't know. I charged up the battery a LOT. So . . ." Rahul turned to Amy. Her face was hopeful. He blinked. "We should be OK. I guess."

"Let ME press it!" said Janet, reaching over from the back.

"Ow! Now your wings are in MY face!" said Amy.

"NO! Don't press it, Janet! That button will make

132

the car go really fast. At the moment, right into the garage door!"

"Oh," said Janet. "Yes."

She sat back again.

"Ow!" said Jack.

"Maybe you *should* take the wings off now, Janet," said Amy.

"Hmm," said Janet, as if thinking, *Maybe I will, but don't blame me when the wings might be needed and I won't be wearing them.*

"So . . ." said Jack, "you know, three minutes ago, that thing I said about this being jokes? So far it's not as much as I thought it might be."

Amy tutted. "Rahul. Open the garage door. Please."

Rahul reached into his pocket and took out a remote control – a *new* remote control.

"I will. And don't worry. I've overhauled the whole system. This will definitely open the door the whole way now." He looked round. "OK . . . are we all ready? Seat belts on?"

"This thing's got seat belts?" said Jack.

"Yes – can't you see yours?"

"Ah yes. It's under a bit of wing."

"Right," said Rahul, "I'm pressing the remote button. Good luck, everyone. And remember – quiet as possible as we go out of the garage and out of the drive – we don't want to wake up my parents . . ."

Everyone nodded. Janet, slightly needlessly, raised her finger to her lips and went "SHHHHHHH!" really loudly.

Rahul's finger hit the button. The garage door began to move up slowly. It looked like this time it was definitely going to go the whole way up.

Unfortunately, it did.

Because just as it got high enough up for the Taylor TurboChaser to get out, the door, whose hinges had clearly not stretched quite this far for a while, started to make a screeching noise. A screeching noise that was less like a garage door opening and more like someone torturing a hundred bats. A hundred bats with microphones.

"WHAT IS THAT NOISE?" shouted Jack.

"SHHHHH!" said Janet.

"THERE'S NO POINT IN SAYING 'SHHHH', TINKERBELL!"

"WHAT?" said Janet.

"STOP THE DOOR MOVING, RAHUL!" shouted Amy.

"I CAN'T!" shouted Rahul.

There was a lot of shouting. Which probably didn't make the noise level any lower. Lights went on in the flat above Agarwal Supplies – the flat where Rahul's family lived.

"Oh dear . . ." he said.

"WHAT ARE WE GOING TO DO?" said Janet. And then, "SHHHHH" to herself.

Amy's face set in a determined way. Jack, looking over, thought, *Hmm, I've seen that face before.*

But before he'd even finished having that thought, Amy had leant over, put her hand into the box in the dashboard and pressed the red turbo button.

"WHAT IS GOING ON?" came Sanjay's voice. Rahul looked up to see his dad leaning out of the window of their flat in his pyjamas.

"HOLD ON TIGHT!" shouted Amy. And she pushed the lever forward as far as it would go.

"*Aaarggghh!*" screamed everyone, as the car catapulted forward, much, much faster than anyone was expecting.

Chapter 20

Trowch i'r chwith

"Where am I going?" said Amy.

"Away from the warehouse door!" said Rahul.

"OK!" she said, sweeping the car left – AAARGGGHH!" went the other three again, as they swung across the seats that way. "But then what?" She hung on as they rounded a couple of corners, faster than she'd like, the whole car leaning to one side, then the other.

"Remember the brake!"

"Oh yes!"

She pressed on the brake button. The car slowed down instantly and stopped on the edge of the industrial estate. An actual road lay ahead.

"Where do I go out of here?" said Amy.

"Start the sat nav," said Rahul. "It's got your dad's work address in Scotland already preloaded."

Amy turned it on. The screen lit up. And said:

"Trowch i'r chwith!"

"Pardon?" said Amy.

"Trowch i'r chwith!"

"Is it speaking backwards?" said Janet.

"Sounds Welsh," said Jack.

"Yeah . . ." said Rahul. "It is. It's faulty. The voice command offers you a number of languages. But this one's stuck on Welsh."

"Brilliant," said Amy.

"RAHUL! WHAT ARE YOU DOING!"

They looked round. Sanjay had come outside, with Rahul's mother, Prisha, who were both in dressing gowns and just looking very confused.

"*Trowch i'r chwith!*" said the sat nav.

"What does it mean?" said Amy.

"I think it means give up now, this is never going to work," said Jack.

"Do you speak Welsh?" said Rahul.

"Oh my," said Jack, "this is going to be a long journey."

"RAHUL! GET OUT OF THAT THING!" shouted Rahul's mother.

"There's a picture, on the sat nav screen," said Janet, pointing. "With arrows."

Amy did a double-take.

"You mean a map.

Of course there is! Thank you, Janet. Now, *I'm* the stupid one!"

"Pardon?" said Janet.

"Nothing," said Amy. She peered at the screen. "Left! It means turn left!"

"*Trowch i'r chwith!*," said Jack. "Obvious."

Amy swung the steering wheel left, and the car moved into the road. It was dark. But then she clicked the light switch and the blackness in front of her lit up. She moved the direction lever gently forward.

"Oh my days," she said. "We're off!"

Jack was looking round. "Not for long. Rahul's mum and dad are getting into their car. They're going to chase us! And, I imagine, fairly soon catch us!"

Rahul shook his head. "No, they won't."

"Why not?"

"I know my mum and dad. Very law-abiding."

Behind them, in their car, Rahul's mum turned to his dad. "Come on, Sanjay! Why are you not starting the car! They are driving away! Rahul and his friends are driving that strange thing away! In the middle of the night!"

"Prisha, have you put your seat belt on?"

"Oh! No. Sorry . . . Where is it?"

"Good question."

They both looked around for a while for their seat belts. And then, when they realised their seat belts weren't *there* any more, they both looked out, to see the back of the Taylor TurboChaser driving away.

Chapter 21

That's nice

For a while, everything was fine. Amy drove along the road, the lights, which were brighter than she expected, illuminating the way in the darkness.

Amy found that by carefully adjusting the direction lever back and forth, she could make the TurboChaser go at a constant, not-too-fast speed. Every so often another car would come past, and the driver would frown at them, but then, because this was a big city and all sorts could be seen on the roads, they would forget about it immediately and just drive on. It felt incredible to be driving along an actual road. The sat nav kept on barking out orders in Welsh, because Rahul had programmed it to take the route with the least possible traffic, so they had to take quiet little back roads. Plus there was hardly anyone about because it was night. But still, it was all so exciting.

In fact, for a while, it looked like Rahul had thought of everything. For example: within five minutes, spatters appeared on the glass in front of Amy.

"Oh no," she said, "it's starting to rain!"

"Don't worry. Click forward on the indicator stick!"

She did. And immediately, outside the glass, what looked to Amy like a bendy kitchen mop appeared, and ran across the wet glass, soaking it up.

"Is that . . ."

"A bendy kitchen mop? Yes."

"A windscreen wiper! Amazing!"

And then:

"I'm cold!" came a voice from the back – Janet.

"Hmm. Wonder if that could be anything to do

with the decision to wear a fairy costume. With no sleeves?" said Jack.

"I think it probably is something to do with that, actually," said Rahul.

"I'm cold!" she said again.

"Don't worry." Rahul reached for a circular dial in front of him. It was a plastic one, and round it had been placed an arc of coloured tape: first blue, then red. He turned the dial so that it faced the red.

Out of the floor behind the front seats, in between Jack and Janet, emerged a pole. At the top of the pole was a black hair dryer.

"Can you switch it on?" said Rahul. "It's battery-powered. But I haven't worked out how to do that from the front."

Jack blinked in amazement. But after a bit of fiddling around the handle to find the switch, he did so.

"Arrgh!" he said, getting a blast of hot air in his

face. He closed his eyes.

"Sorry. You need to give it a slap."

"What? I can't hear you! It's still blowing in my face!"

"Give it a slap!"

Jack did so.

"Ow! You just hit me!" said Janet.

"Sorry!" said Jack. "I can't see."

Janet tutted, and slapped the hair dryer herself. It started to revolve.

"*Aaaahhh . . .*" she said, when it got round to her, "that's nice."

Rahul beamed with pride. He pointed to the dial. "Heating system."

Amy nodded. She pointed at the blue bit of tape. "It can go cold as well?"

Rahul shook his head. "No. That's just to look right."

"I see," she said.

The journey seemed to really be going much

more easily than Amy had thought it might do. She even decided to say this out loud.

"It's going much more easily than I thought it might do. If everything carries on like this, we'll be in Scotland by the morning!" She looked at her watch. It was 1:30am on Saturday morning. Dad wasn't leaving for Japan till Sunday. Loads of time!

"Yeah! Definitely!" said Jack.

Amy didn't like the sound of that. Jack never said *anything* positive – unless he was being sarcastic.

"Because one thing Rahul's parents will definitely do," continued Jack, proving her right, "is sit in the car and just wait for us to come back. And not ring our mum, or anything . . ."

Amy's stomach fell.

Rahul frowned, and shook his head. "No, I think they *might* do that."

Chapter 22

Something you might see in a cartoon

"So, Mrs Taylor," said DCI Bryant, sipping the tea that Suzi had made for him. They were sitting in the Taylors' kitchen, round their small breakfast table. It was the very early hours of Saturday morning. "Your daughter is disabled . . . ?"

"Yes. She had an accident a few years ago and broke her back. Now she can't use her legs."

"What kind of accident . . . ?"

Suzi's face, already clouded with worry, turned

even darker. "Her father was driving. It wasn't his fault. Another car was on the wrong side of the road and . . . anyway, do you need to know all the details of that? Will it help find her?"

DCI Bryant blinked. "No. I guess not. I'm sorry to intrude on a painful memory."

Suzi nodded.

"I imagine it *was* painful, though," said PC Middleton.

Suzi looked over. PC Middleton was standing by, his notepad in hand.

"PC Middleton . . ." said DCI Bryant wearily.

"A car crash . . . Ow!"

Suzi frowned. "That's not quite what 'painful' means in that—"

"Don't bother, Mrs Taylor," said DCI Bryant even more wearily.

"I think it may be more important to tell you about the car, Mr Bryant," said Sanjay, who was also sitting round the table, as were Prisha, and Colin and Norma Warner, Janet's parents. It was pretty cramped. Not least because Colin and Norma were both happy to spread themselves out on their chairs.

"The one they went away in," Sanjay added.

"The car? The children were kidnapped by someone driving a car?"

"No, no, no!" said Prisha. "*She* was driving the car! Amy!"

DCI Bryant turned to Suzi. "Your daughter, a *child*, was driving a car?"

"It ain't a *car*, you big wazzock!" said Colin.

"No, it ain't! Wazzock!" said Norma.

"Excuse me," said PC Middleton. "Please moderate your language, sir and madam. Do NOT call the Detective Inspector a wazzock."

"Oh! What will you charge us with, then?"

"Yeah, charge us with what?"

"Saying the word 'wazzock' in a built-up area?"

"Ha ha ha ha, yeah, a built-up area!"

This seemed to be mainly what Colin and Norma did: what some people call "bantz". Even though their daughter had gone missing.

"I should inform you, Mr and Mrs Warner, that I have written that down," said PC Middleton.

"Anyway," said DCI Bryant, "this car. Vehicle. Whatever. The thing Amy was driv—"

"Sir . . . would you know how many Zs there are in 'wazzock'?"

"Twelve!" said Norma.

"Yeah, twelve!" said Colin.

PC Middleton scribbled on his pad, then frowned. "That looks a bit strange. Like how you would write down the sound of someone sleeping."

"Stop writing, Middleton," said DCI Bryant.

"Are you sure, sir?"

"Zip it, Middleton! ZIP IT!"

"Right you are, sir."

DCI Bryant sighed very heavily, and then turned back to Prisha.

"You were saying, Mrs Agarwal . . . ?"

"Yes. Well. Colin and Norma are right, it wasn't a car. At least, not a normal car. It was more like . . . something you might see in a cartoon."

"A cartoon? What kind of cartoon?"

"*The Simpsons? Spongebob? Minions? Tom and Jerry? The Amazing World of Gumball?*"

"Yes. That's enough cartoon examples now, Middleton."

"I don't know," said Prisha. "Sort of like an *old* cartoon that had a car from the future in it."

"*This* is what it's like," said Suzi, holding up her phone. DCI Bryant and PC Middleton peered at it. "It's a photo my son took. I copied it to my phone."

"Oh my goodness . . ." said DCI Bryant.

"Hmmm . . ." said PC Middleton, holding his pencil up to the phone.

"Don't draw it on your pad, Middleton."

"No, sir?"

"No. We have a photo here. So we don't need you to do a drawing."

"Right you are, sir."

"It kind of *is* like a cartoon car from the future in an old cartoon," said DCI Bryant.

"Thank you," said Prisha.

"But it's different now," said Sanjay. "The car. It's bigger and has new bits."

"But does it still look basically like this?" said DCI Bryant.

Sanjay looked at it. He nodded.

"And where do you think it – they – might be going?"

Everyone looked to Suzi. She shook her head, looked down, and then, after a little while, looked up.

"My guess is – even though I don't want it to be true – Scotland. Just past the border, to be exact."

Chapter 23

Road closed

"So, Rahul . . ." said Jack, "we've definitely got enough power to get to Scotland, then?"

They had been going for about an hour. They had managed to stay off big roads and were now almost out of the city.

"Well . . . I think so."

"Oh, that's good," said Jack.

"Yes, it is."

"No, Rahul," Amy said. "That's Jack being sarcastic."

"Oh. Is it not good?"

"Well, Rahul," said Jack. "I'd prefer you to *know* that we've got enough power. Rather than *think* it."

"Oh, I see. Well, no, I don't. Especially not now that you're with us."

"*Parhewch am filltir . . .*"

"Thank you, sat nav," said Jack. "That's very helpful."

Amy tutted, leant over and banged the sat nav screen with her fist.

"CONTINUE FOR A MILE!" said the sat nav.

"Oh my!" said Janet.

"A MILE! CONTINUE!"

"You fixed it!" said Rahul. "It speaks English now!"

"Yeah!" said Amy.

"CONTINUE! DO NOT TURN OFF!"

"I seem to have made it change personality at the same time."

"STAY ON THIS ROAD!"

"OK! OMG!"

"Actually," said Rahul, "I don't think we can."

Amy looked ahead. They had been travelling on a small, dark lane. As they approached the end of it, a sign appeared:

"STAY. ON. THIS. ROAD!" said the sat nav.

"We can't!" shouted Amy, putting on the brake. They screeched to a stop, right by the sign.

"Oh dear," said Jack.

"CONTINUE!"

"Can we turn that off?" said Janet.

Amy banged the screen again with her fist.

"*CYNNWYS!*" said the sat nav.

Amy frowned.

"I think that might be 'continue' in Welsh," said Rahul.

"Shall we just go round the sign?" said Amy.

"Um . . . we don't know what's there. I don't think it's a good idea. It might be an enormous hole in the road."

"What are we going to do, Rahul?" said Amy.

"We could get a Welsh–English dictionary?"

"No," said Amy, "to carry on with the journey."

"Are we going home, then?" said Janet.

"Yes," said Jack. "But *you* have to fly there."

In response, Janet flapped her wings. In Jack's face.

"Ow!"

"OK," said Rahul. "We could turn round. But it's a long way back to the next road we can take. And Jack is right, I don't know that we've got enough power as it is. So . . . there's a field next to us, isn't there?"

Everyone looked over.

"Um . . ." said Amy, "I think so. It's very dark."

Rahul rummaged in his bag and took out a torch. He turned it on and pointed the beam towards the window. It wasn't really a window, it was just his section of the glass that made up the roof of the Taylor TurboChaser. But it's easier to call it a window.

Four pairs of eyes looked out at the darkness, illuminated in patches as Rahul moved the torch along. And then four mouths went . . .

"AAAAAAARRRGGH!"

. . . as the beam lit up a pair of eyes staring back at them.

Chapter 24

APB

"OK," said DCI Bryant. He was standing by his police car, outside Amy's house. "Thanks for all the information. We've put out an APB, and—"

"Oooh, APB! Oooh, hello, Kojak!" said Norma. "You're going to put out a Code Red as well?"

"Watch out, Colombo!" said Colin.

"What are they saying now, sir?" said PC Middleton.

"They are referring to old television detectives,

Middleton. As a way of making fun of me," said DCI Bryant wearily.

"I see. How do you spell 'Colomb—'"

"Don't write it down."

"Are you going to give us a quick CSI as well?" said Colin.

"Ha ha ha, CSI!" said Norma.

"I'll be giving you an ASBO in a minute . . ."

That did, in fact quieten Colin and Norma down very quickly.

"Thank you." Then, to PC Middleton, over some

whispering from them, "It means 'Anti-Social Behaviour Order'." He turned back to the parents. "APB, meanwhile, means 'All Police Bulletin'. I've sent the picture of the vehicle to our central computer. Which means, in turn, that it will be sent to all police cars presently on the main roads between here and Scotland. So as soon as they are spotted, which I'm sure won't be long, this will all be over."

He sounded very reassuring. Although the parents didn't look very reassured.

"Right. And what should we do?" said Suzi.

"Well . . ." said DCI Bryant, "just wait in your homes. We will inform you as soon as your children are apprehended."

And with that, they got in the car and drove off.

Suzi looked round

"Are we going to do that? Stay in our homes and just wait? Or are we going to get in my car and look for them ourselves?"

"We are!" said Prisha.

"Er . . ." said Sanjay. "Shouldn't we do what the policeman says and—" And then following a very steely glance from his wife: "No, of course. Yes. We are."

"BRING IT ON!" said Norma.

"What, the ASBO?" said Colin.

Chapter 25

Like the cheese in a sandwich

"**A**AAAARGGGGGH!"
shouted the four children in the Taylor
TurboChaser, a second time.

It was a loud shout, so it was quite difficult
to hear, just underneath the end of it, a different
sound. But Amy, who had very good hearing,
did.

"AARRGGH . . . Sorry, what was
that?" she said.

"AAAAARRGGH . . . what?" said
Rahul.

"AAAAAAARRGGG—" said Janet.

"Shush, Janet!" said Amy.

". . . GGGGHHHH – OK," said Janet.

There was a sudden quiet in the car. Rahul flashed
the torch towards the side again. Once again, the
eyes. But this time, because no one screamed, there
was something noticeable about them. They weren't
staring, aggressive, hard eyes. They were lazy eyes.

Soft eyes. They blinked. Lazily, softly. And then the sound again.

"*Moooooooo* . . ."

"Oh," said Amy. "It's a cow."

Rahul flicked the torch across. "Cows. Loads of them. They're all staring at us!"

"AAAAAARRGHHH!" said Janet.

"No, it's not really a problem, Janet," said Rahul.

"Oh, right."

"Except you're saying we should go through the field, aren't you, Rahul?" said Jack.

"Um. Oh. Yes! I *was* suggesting that. Before we started screaming."

"So . . . through the cows?"

Rahul turned to Amy.

"Are you OK with that?"

"Hmm . . ."

"Remember how you slalomed through dustbins on my dad's drive?"

"Yeah. But none of those dustbins had udders. Or hooves. Or the ability to *move*."

"No . . ."

"Plus, will the car be able to deal with a field? I mean . . . it's not designed for that."

Rahul smiled. "Well, you say that, but . . ."

He reached over. In between the two of them was what looked like an electric pump. Which indeed it was. Amy had assumed it was there in case they got a flat tyre. But it turned out it had another purpose.

Rahul switched it on. Nothing, apart from a

whooshing sound, happened for a second. And then:

"*Whooa!*" said Jack.

"What's happening?" said Amy.

"WHY ARE WE GOING UP?" said Janet.

"It's an inflatable mattress. I put it underneath the chassis."

"THE SHASSY? WHAT'S THE SHASSY?"

"The floor of the car, Janet. It's stuck in between the two bits that make up the floor of the car, like the meat in a sandwich."

"I'm a vegetarian!" said Amy.

"OK. The *cheese* in a sandwich."

"WE'RE GOING UP REALLY HIGH!"

"About twelve centimetres higher than before, Janet." Rahul turned to Amy "Welcome to the Taylor TurboChaser four-by-four."

Chapter 26

Strange-looking cow

Amy took a deep breath. The way Rahul had designed the TurboChaser to fit any situation, with all his little add-ons, was incredible, but she was still the one who had to drive it.

And even if he had somehow been expecting that they might have to drive through a field, she had not.

Certainly not a field of cows.

But there seemed to be little choice, except turning back and giving up. Amy was not going to do that. So she turned the steering wheel to the left and pushed the direction lever forward, driving towards where, as the lights on the front of the vehicle showed, a small track led to the field. Of cows.

"Take it slowly," said Jack.

"Thanks, Jeremy Clarkson," said Amy.

They went through on to the grass. She could feel how different it was straight away – the car rolled and dragged, the tyres slipping and sliding over the damp terrain. It was harder to control.

"Um . . . where am I going?"

Rahul hit the screen.

"OH MY GOD! YOU'VE GONE OFF ROAD! I HAVE NO IDEA WHERE YOU ARE! WHAT'S GOING ON?"

"Hmm," said Rahul, "something seems to have happened to the sat nav."

"TURN BACK! JUST STOP! PLEASE! THERE COULD BE COWS IN HERE AND EVERYTHING!"

Rahul hit it again.

"*Parhewch am filltir . . .*"

"Ah . . . what did that mean again?" said Amy.

"Continue for a mile," said Jack.

"Thank you."

"Happy to help."

"OK. I'll just go in as straight a line as I ca—
AAARGH!"

That AAARGH was because, in the middle of
the line of straightness she was trying to go in, was
a cow, quite clearly lit by the bright moon and the
headlights.

For those of you interested in cows, it was a Friesian, with black patches on a mainly white body. But really all you need to know is that suddenly there was a big wall of leather, and they were heading right towards it.

Amy swerved to the right, where there was another cow, staring at her in a kind of "this is interesting" way. She swerved again. Everyone in the car screamed. Her hand moved the direction lever forward, slowly, making the engine roar, but without moving forward.

"Why are you revving up?" shouted Jack. "I said take it slowly!"

"I'm trying to get away from the cows! Plus if you knew anything about driving, you'd know I can't drive too slowly on this grass! We'd get stuck!"

"*We'd get stuck!*" said Jack sarcastically.

"Yes, we would, actually," said Rahul, which made

Jack shut up quite quickly, because, cool and sarcastic fourteen-year-old or not, he really didn't want to get stuck in this field in the middle of the night.

Amy swung the car left, then right, slaloming like she had through the dustbins, but now through the cows. It was a great piece of driving, and she seemed to have got them through the field safely. Most of the cows just watched them go by, glad to have something a little bit different going on to break up the evening.

But suddenly . . .

"OK," said Rahul, pointing. "If you go through that gap in the hedge there, we'll be through this field, and we can go out to the road beyond—"

"What's that noise?" said Jack.

"Sorry, that was me," said Janet. "I had beans for dinner."

"No, not that noise – *that* one; the one that sounds like snarling. And panting."

"It's that!" said Amy, pointing directly in front of them.

Janet and Jack leant over from the back.

Lit up by their own headlights, and by the powerful light of the moon, was another pair of eyes, only this time angry, staring, not friendly. Below the eyes was a wide black nose, pierced with an enormous metal ring; and, above, a set of large, sharp horns.

"Hmm. That's a strange-looking cow," said Janet.

Chapter 27

Not right at all

"**B**ull, Janet," said Amy.

"Don't be rude. It IS a strange-looking cow."

"No, I mean—"

"OK," said Jack quietly. "The thing to do is just be very, very quie—"

"*And* it's in our way . . ." Janet continued, leaning over and pressing the air horn.

PAAAAARP!

It really was very loud.

"JANET!" said all three of the others.

"What?" she said, parping it again.

PAAAAARP!

"GET OUT THE WAY, YOU SILLY WEIRD COW!"

The silly weird cow – which, as I think you know, was not a cow – looked very, very angry at the noise.

"IT'S A BULL, JANET!" shouted Amy. "AND . . . IT'S ABOUT TO COME RIGHT FOR US!"

"How do you know that?" said Janet.

"Look!"

The bull had, indeed, started to do that thing that bulls do, of putting its head down and pawing at the ground with one of its front hooves. Which, it's true, generally *doesn't* mean, *"Oh, hi, nice human, please come and give my horns a friendly stroke."*

"WHAT ARE WE GOING TO DO?"

"I've got an idea!" said Rahul. "I can press the hazard button!"

"How will that work? No one's here to even see it!"

"It makes the car into a matador!"

"It makes the car into a doormat?" said Janet.

"No!" said Rahul. "A matador! A bullfighter! You must have seen them on the internet! Men in Spain who wear funny costumes and fight bulls!"

"Oh yes. I don't really approve of them," said Amy, "because it's not a fair fight, and they always end up killing the bulls."

"Can we have the ethical discussion later?" said Jack. "How does pressing the hazard button help?"

Rahul's finger lingered on the button.

"The way the matador dodges the bull is by using a red cape. So −" he pressed the button, and a red flag came out of the back left-hand corner of the TurboChaser − "we'll use our hazard flag as a cape!"

"Erm . . ." said Amy, "don't they also use red because that colour makes bulls—"

"HE'S CHARGING! HE'S CHARGING STRAIGHT AT US! HE LOOKS REALLY ANGRY!" shouted Janet.

"Yes. That would be the word I was looking for," said Amy. She looked at Rahul. "I hope this works . . ."

"So do I," said Rahul.

A thought came into Amy's head: *The first thing you need to do to get over a problem is believe you can.* It was one of her mum's annoying inspirational quotes! What was it doing in her head now?

Although, weirdly, it seemed to help how she felt about the whole situation. It didn't help much. But it helped a little.

She pulled down hard on the steering wheel and threw the direction lever forward. The TurboChaser spun round, so that the hazard flag was facing the bull.

"HE'S STILL CHARGING STRAIGHT AT US!" shouted Janet.

"I HATE TO AGREE WITH JANET, BUT HE IS!" shouted Jack.

"Right," said Amy to Rahul. "I'm going with your matador idea. So when I say *now*, press the hazard button again."

"O–"

"NOOOOWWW!"

Frantically, Rahul pressed the button. The flag flew back in the car, which meant the bull, who had been aiming right for it, ran straight through . . . nothing. And kept going.

"Brilliant, Amy!" said Rahul, looking over his shoulder.

"Thanks!" She looked over her shoulder too. The bull skidded to a halt. It frowned, as if to say, "Eh? What happened?" But then slowly, and with a strong sense of being even more annoyed now, he turned round.

"But I don't think it's over. Let's go!"

Amy threw the direction lever forward. The TurboChaser moved towards the gap in the hedge again. But it took a while to get up to speed on the wet grass, and she could hear the bull approaching.

She could also *see* it approaching in her rear-view mirror.

"IT'S GOING TO SPEAR US FROM BEHIND!" shouted Janet.

With an agonising crash, it did. With a terrible crunch, the bull's horns came into contact with the back of the TurboChaser.

"AAAAARGGGH!" cried Janet and Jack.

Amy reached over and pressed the hazard button again. The red flag popped out once more. The bull, distracted, swerved away from the car towards it.

Amy swung the car in the opposite direction; the bull swung towards it; Amy turned back again; the bull followed. They went round and round in a figure of eight, the bull continually trying to headbutt the hazard flag, Amy continually swerving out of the way at the last minute.

"I know what to do!" said Janet. She took out her phone.

Jack looked at her. "You're going to call the farmer? The RSPCA? A cowboy who might be able to rodeo this monster out of here?"

Janet shook her head, and clicked on her phone. Immediately, music started playing out of the Bluetooth speaker that Rahul had Blu-tacked to the dashboard.

"What. Is. That?" shouted Jack.

"It's a song my mum really likes. 'A Beaver's Banana', I think it's called."

"'Oh, this year I'm off to sunny Spain . . . *Y viva España!*'" came out of the speaker.

"I just thought some Spanish music felt . . . right," Janet continued.

And indeed, had you been perhaps passing that field at that moment, and seen the whole scene from afar, many things about the sight of a weird car with a red flag dodging a chasing bull would not have felt right at all. But something about the music would have done.

"'. . . I'm off to sunny *Spain* . . .'"

Chapter 28

Peter Pat

"**P**hew," said Rahul. "That wasn't easy."

"No," said Amy.

It was ten minutes later. They were driving through the next field, which was, thankfully, free of cows and, more importantly, bulls.

"But you did brilliantly, Amy. You tired him out!"

Jack leant over from the back and put his hand on her shoulder. "Yeah. Well played, sis."

Amy glanced backwards. He still had his sarcastic

face on. But through that she could tell he meant it.

"I tired myself out quite a lot as well, though."

"OMG, what is that smell?" said Jack.

"It's ME!" said Janet.

"Oh, not the bean thing again . . ."

"NO!" said Janet. "LOOK!"

Amy stopped the car. Everyone looked at Janet.

There was no getting round what they were seeing. Her fairy wings were covered, completely, in cow poo.

"HOW DID THAT HAPPEN?" Janet screamed, on the verge of tears.

"I think . . ." said Rahul, looking at the glass behind her, "it came through there."

They all looked round. A crack had appeared, running all the way along the glass at the back of the car.

"Oh dear," said Amy. "It must have shot up from the ground when we were skidding around."

"*Urrrggghhh*," said Janet.

"Maybe, Janet, at last, this *might* be a reason to take the wings off?" said Jack. "Or were you hoping to fly to meet Peter Pat?"

"His name is Pan," said Rahul.

"PETER PAT! AS IN COW PAT! IT'S A JOKE!" shouted Jack.

Rahul thought about this for a second, then nodded. "I see. I think 'To meet Mr Smee-ly' would've been better."

"Oh, now you're the King of the Comedy Workshop, Rahul?"

"OK, calm down, everyone," said Amy. "I think you *are* going to have to get rid of the wings, Janet. It does smell like the inside of a cow's stomach in here."

"They have four stomachs, you know," said Rahul.

"Yeah," said Jack. "All of them poo-ey."

"We should stop, Amy," said Rahul. "I'm going

to have to check out how bad that crack is. And we should clean the car up a bit."

"But . . ." said Amy, "I really wanted to try and get there in one night."

"Yes. I think that may have been a bit ambitious."

"I'm that!" said Janet.

"You are?" said Jack.

"Yes. I can write with my left AND my right hand!"

"You mean 'ambidextrous'," said Amy.

Jack looked at Janet. "I'm just amazed you can write at all, Janet."

Janet looked at him.

"U.U.R.G.G.H. What does that spell, Jack?"

"Pardon?" he said.

Janet flicked one shoulder forward. Which flicked one wing forward. Which flicked a large sliver of cow poo at Jack's face.

"UURGGH!" he said.

"Correct," said Janet.

"OK," said Amy. "It's still early on Saturday morning. We've got loads of time to get to Scotland. Let's stop here for a bit."

Chapter 29

Good meme

Amy found a spot at the edge of the field under a large oak tree, and parked. Rahul got out of the TurboChaser with his torch, and began scraping at the back window with a spatula.

"There's a lot of cow mess on here!" he shouted.

"Oh, that is good," said Jack.

"It *is* good!" said Rahul. "We can use it for—"

"I don't even want to know what for, thanks," said Jack, getting out of the car. "Would you like the bits on my face too?"

Rahul shone the torch at him and squinted. "No. That's just some flecks. It's not enough."

Janet appeared next to Jack.

"Is there anywhere to wash this off?"

Rahul flashed the torch towards the oak tree.

"There's a little stream, I think, down behind the tree."

They went down there.

"Sorry," said Janet to Jack, as she took her wings and dipped them in the water.

"That's OK," said Jack, splashing his face. "Good meme."

"What was?"

"The poo-flick, spell-URRGH joke."

Janet beamed. "Thanks!"

Meanwhile, Amy called over to Rahul from her seat.

"What about the crack in the window?"

"I've put some black tape on it. I think it will hold up until we get there . . . What about you?"

"How do you mean?"

Rahul looked at her. "Will you hold up until we get there? This is hard work."

Amy blinked. She felt that she was, already, deeply tired. She looked at the alarm clock on the dashboard: it was three o'clock in the morning.

"I'll do my best," she said.

Janet and Jack came back from the stream.

"OK, everyone!" Amy said. "Try and get some sleep. We'll get going again as soon as it's light tomorrow."

"Will it be OK to drive during the day? Won't people think, *What kind of car is that*?" said Janet.

"I've had an idea about that," said Rahul.

"Where are we going to sleep?" said Jack.

"In the car," said Rahul.

"In the car?" repeated Jack, and not sarcastically, just astonished.

"I've had an idea about that too," said Rahul. "Well, I had an idea about it, in advance. I thought we might have to sleep in it, so . . . Amy, can you press that button on the dashboard, the one that looks like a teepee?"

Amy looked down. She pressed it. Nothing happened.

"Nothing's happening" she shouted.

"Just wait," said Rahul.

He went over to the front of the car. He bent down to the TAYTURB1 number plate and lifted it up. He rummaged around underneath and pulled out a crank handle, a bit like the ones on very old cars that people in the very old days would turn round and round to get the engine going. And that, in fact, was what Rahul did. He turned the crank round and round. But it didn't start the engine.

Instead, out of the chimney, the one that poked through a cat flap in the roof, came a fabric of many different colours – red, blue, green, yellow – shooting out like a kind of cloth firework. It fell over the car, like a loose drape. Then he turned the handle the other way, and the material tightened and moved upwards, making the car into . . .

"A tent!" said Amy. "You've made it into a tent!"

"Yes," said Rahul. "And I packed sleeping bags!"

With the tent round it, inside the TurboChaser everything felt very cosy. Amy switched on some of the car lights so that they could see. Rahul showed them how to fold down the glass sides of the inside of the car to make an enormous bed for them all to sleep in. A comfortable bed, because he was also able to slide out the mattresses from beneath the chassis for them to sleep on. They all got into sleeping bags (courtesy of Agarwal Supplies, Outdoor Section). Then Janet brought out her Lodlil bag.

"Dinner!" she said.

"Yum! Lovely!" said Rahul. "What is it?"

She turned her bag upside down. About forty plastic cartons rolled out.

"Beans! Baked beans!"

Amy, Jack and Rahul looked at each other.

"And . . . ?" said Jack.

"Four plastic forks!" said Janet, fishing them out of the bag.

Amy shook her head, and laughed. She grabbed a fork and peeled open a carton.

"Nothing like cold beans!" she said.

"That's what people say about leftovers. After they've been hot," said Jack, picking up a fork wearily. "Not about ones that have never been heated at all . . ."

"Yum," said Janet, her mouth full.

After dinner, they all settled down to sleep. It was warm, and dark, and Amy felt especially tired – she did, after all, have to drive all by herself, and just with her arms.

"Goodnight, everybody!" she said.

"Goodnight, Amy!" said Rahul.

"Night, sis. Good meme," said Jack.

"Night, um, bro," said Amy.

She was asleep before she noticed that Janet

hadn't said anything. In fact, they were all asleep, and so couldn't hear a tap-tap-tapping sound coming from her sleeping bag.

Chapter 30

SAVE ME!

"How long are we going to wait here, Mrs Taylor?"

"Be quiet, Sanjay."

"I'm sorry, Prisha, my love. Only . . . I have a big delivery coming tomorrow for the warehouse. And I was hoping to get some sleep before then."

Suzi, who was driving the van, had pulled over. They were in a layby, somewhere off the long motorway that winds from the city up to the north. Prisha was in the passenger seat. Sanjay and Norma and Colin were in the back.

Norma and Colin were sleeping on each other's shoulders. Colin was dribbling a little.

"I don't know, is the answer, Sanjay. I just have no idea where to start with finding them. This is a very long road and there are a lot of cars on it. And we don't even know if this is the way they came."

"How can you sleep, Sanjay," said Prisha, turning round, "when you know our child is out there somewhere on the roads in . . . in . . .?"

"The Taylor TurboChaser."

"The what?"

"The Taylor TurboChaser. That's what they call it."

"Yes," said Suzi. "It is."

"It is nice, at least, that Rahul named it after your family," said Sanjay.

Suzi sighed, and half smiled. "Yes. Lovely thought. But right now I'd prefer just to know where it is."

BLEEP! BLEEP! came a noise from the back.

"OH LORDY! HELP ME! SAVE ME! NOT THE DEMENTORS!"

"COLIN! IT'S OK! YOU WERE HAVING THAT NIGHTMARE AGAIN!"

BLEEP! BLEEP!

"Norma, I think it's your mobile," said Suzi.

"Oh. OK. You stupid banana, Colin."

"I didn't have my Patronus, Norma. It was sucking the life out of me!"

"Shh. Oh look."

"What?" said Suzi.

"It's a text from Janet."

Sanjay, Prisha and Suzi looked round, wide-eyed and open-mouthed.

"Oh," said Colin. "What's it say?"

Chapter 31

I'm not an idiot

Amy awoke to a whooshing sound. It was Rahul outside the TurboChaser winding up the tent. The coloured cloth was funnelling back inside the chimney. Which meant that Amy suddenly felt a bit exposed, lying on some glass plates in the open air in the middle of a field.

She rubbed her eyes. "What time is it?"

"Go away," said Jack, who normally said that when woken up. In fact, he normally said it over and over again, until forced out of bed much later by Suzi.

Amy looked out. The sun, which had come up a while ago, was bright against a blue morning sky. The field they were in was very green. In her vision, Rahul suddenly appeared, holding something rolled up. It looked like a poster.

"What is that?" said Amy.

Rahul unrolled it. It was a long piece of paper, more like a banner than a poster. On it he had written:

He had drawn a series of doodles round these words, of various crazy-looking cars.

Amy nodded. Then she said, "I'll ask again. What is that?"

"I've made up an event," said Rahul. "The Crazy Car Rally!"

"And . . . ?"

"And if I put this up somewhere on the car, people who see us on the road will think, *Oh right, I see. It's a crazy car going to some sort of crazy car event.* And then they won't think about it any more. It's sort of like an invisibility cloak. Except not."

"OK, I get it! Brilliant, clever!"

"Thanks!" said Rahul, and he started attaching the banner to the front of the car.

"Why so many exclamation marks?" said Amy.

"That's what you do if you're the kind of person who goes to the Crazy Car Rally. You use a lot of exclamation marks. To show how crazy you are."

"Right. I'll bear that in mind. OK, I think we should be getting on. Jack!"

"Go away."

"No, come on."

"What's for breakfast?"

"Um . . . more of Janet's beans?"

"Go away."

Rahul started folding up the glass plates. Which involved rolling Jack over on his side.

"I said *go away.*"

Amy sighed. "OK, we'll come back to you. Janet!"

Janet popped her head out of her sleeping bag.

"I was awake already. Just under the covers!"

"Great," said Amy.

"Because it's easier to see your phone there. It's too light out here."

"Right. You've got a signal here?"

"Some of the time . . . Anyone for beans?"

BLEEP! BLEEP!

Janet dived back into her sleeping bag.

"Well . . ." said Rahul. "Jack's still asleep . . ."

"I'm not."

"Oh."

"Go away."

"Right. But I've folded up the car, the tent material has gone back into the chimney – so we could have breakfast and then—"

"Janet . . ." said Amy, who had spent the last few minutes thinking and frowning at Janet's sleeping bag.

"Yes . . ." she said, muffled, from inside it.

"Who are you texting?"

"Mum and Dad!" she said.

Rahul, who was getting into the passenger seat, stopped and looked at her. Jack, who had his eyes closed and had been doing his very best not to wake up properly, opened them, and sat up.

"Er, since when?" said Jack.

"Well, I sent them a text last night," said Janet. "But they haven't replied yet, so—"

"Oh no," said Rahul.

"What?" said Janet.

And Amy said:

"And . . . what are you *saying* in your message now?"

Janet's head came out of the sleeping bag again. "Don't worry! Just that we're OK, and having a great time being chased by bulls and stuff. I'm not telling them where we are! I'm not an idiot. Actually, where are we?"

"I'm not entirely sure," said Rahul.

"But you could probably find out," said Jack, "from Location Services on your phone. As could anyone who's in contact with your phone. Certainly anyone who, I don't know, *bought* your phone for you and has access to your account."

"Not to mention," said Rahul, "anyone who's had a message since *last night*. So could have been tracking us for a while."

There was a pause. Janet frowned at him. Then she looked at her phone.

"Oops," she said.

Chapter 32

Waving goodbye

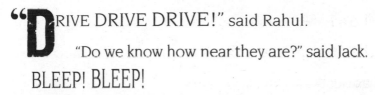

"**D**RIVE DRIVE DRIVE!" said Rahul.

"Do we know how near they are?" said Jack.

BLEEP! BLEEP!

"Oh," said Janet. "It's them! It says, DO NOT MOVE. WE ARE COMING TO GET YOU. WE WILL BE THERE IN AN HOUR."

"DRIVE DRIVE DRIVE!" said Rahul.

Five minutes later, they were on the road. Not just on their way, which is what "on the road" can sometimes mean, but actually on a proper road again, no longer driving through fields. It was only a country lane, but, still, there were other cars on it, which meant that they were getting some very funny looks from passing drivers.

Although one, at least, shouted out: "Enjoy the Crazy Car Rally!"

"You're going to have to turn your phone off, Janet!" said Amy.

"What?" said Janet anxiously.

"You are," said Rahul.

"But I won't text them any more," she said more anxiously.

"It doesn't matter," said Jack. "If your phone's on, they'll be able to trace us."

"But I never turn my phone off!" Janet said, looking as anxious as she possibly could.

"What about when it runs out of power?" said Jack.

"I make sure it never runs out of power!"

"How?"

"By keeping it plugged in!"

"Where?"

"In a power point!"

"Right. Janet . . . how can I put this?" said Jack. "Right now, are we in a house? With power points? Or are we in . . . a ridiculous contraption, sort of a car, sort of a fish tank on wheels, but definitely without power points?"

"Actually . . ." said Rahul, "I could probably fix up a—"

"DON'T OFFER HER A POWER SOURCE!" said Amy.

"OK," said Rahul.

"Seriously, Janet, you're going to have to turn your phone off," said Amy.

"ALL RIGHT! ALL RIGHT!" shouted Janet.

She held her phone up in the air. Her thumb

hovered over the "off" button. Her eyes appeared to
fill with tears.

"Goodbye," she whispered.

"Really," said Jack. "I think it's *au revoir*."

"I don't speak German," said Janet.

"It's—"

"Jack!" said Amy. "Let her turn it off!"

"Let her turn it off," he repeated, in his most stupid
voice.

Janet held up the phone again.

"Goodbye . . . I love you . . ."

"Oh my days," said Jack.

"Shh," said Amy.

Closing her eyes, Janet pressed her thumb against the side of the phone. The screen went to a smiley-face icon, with little hands, waving goodbye. Janet, who had clearly never seen it before, waved back, brushing away the tears that had now come.

The screen went black.

"AAARGH! AAAAAARRRGGH!" screamed Janet. "MY PHONE, MY PHONE!"

"WHY HAST THOU FORSAKEN ME?" said Jack.

"Anyway," said Amy, looking ahead. "We've got another problem."

Chapter 33

Via Big Fart Moor

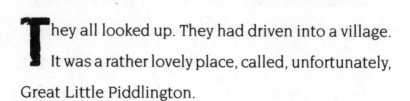

They all looked up. They had driven into a village. It was a rather lovely place, called, unfortunately, Great Little Piddlington.

"Ha ha ha ha!" said Jack. "Great Little Piddlington!"

"Yes, hugely funny," said Amy. "But also, hugely long traffic jam, up ahead."

Amy put the brakes on. The TurboChaser stopped.

"Well, not up ahead any more. We are in the traffic jam."

Rahul rummaged under his seat. He got out a pair of binoculars with a telescope stuck to them.

"What's that?" said Jack.

"It's called a Binocuscope."

"When did you make that?"

"I didn't. I bought it off Sam Green. He made it." Rahul put his head through his cat flap and put the Binocuscope to his eyes. Then he came back in again.

"I think there're some sort of roadworks in the middle of the village. It looks like they go on forever!"

"Try the sat nav. Maybe there's a different way?"

"Or I could turn my phone back on and look at the map?"

"No, it's OK, Janet," said Amy. She hit the sat nav screen.

"YOU'RE IN A TRAFFIC JAM! TURN ROUND! PLEASE! SAVE YOURSELF! ETA AT YOUR DESTINATION IS NOW MONDAY AFTERNOON!"

"Monday afternoon?" said Jack. "That's far too late!"

"Yes. Also, what *is* that voice setting?" said Amy, and she hit it again.

"Hi," said the sat nav smoothly. This voice sounded a bit like a middle-aged DJ on a local radio station.

"Oh, this is a new one," said Jack.

"Lovely to be directing you. I see you're in a bit of a pickle. No worries . . ."

"It's a nice voice. It's making me feel like everything's going to be OK," said Amy.

"That's great! So . . . what you need to do, OK, is take the next right, and continue to Large Bottom."

"HA HA HA HA!" went all the children in the car.

"Please don't laugh – I mean, I get it, Large Bottom . . ."

"HA HA HA HA!"

". . . Ha ha ha, funny – but really it's just the name

of the next village. So from Large Bottom . . ."

"HA HA HA HA!"

". . . take a left towards Little Smell Hole . . ."

"HA HA HA HA HA!"

". . . then go straight up the Wobbly Nud-Nuds . . ."

"HA HA HA HA HA!"

"It's a series of hills! I mean, really! Come on!"

The children quietened down.

"Thank you. Yes. Good. And then . . . everyone fine? . . . OK. Take the A312 all the way to Stinky Nickers," it continued, "via Big Fart Moor, Nappy Town, Thrice-Widdle, Lower Widdle, Widdle Widdle, Last Little Widdle and Plopton."

"HA HA HA HA HA HA HA HA HA HA HA HA HA HA HA HA HA!"

"Oh, for heaven's sake, find your own stupid way!" said the sat nav, and turned itself off.

"Hmm . . ." said Amy. "I think we might have to find a different method of beating this traffic jam."

"Have we moved in the last ten minutes?" said Jack.

"Only with laughter."

"Oh no," said Amy, who suddenly remembered it was now Saturday, and they needed to be there by Sunday. "It's getting on for midday. Time is slipping by."

"We could try this," said Rahul.

"What?"

"Here." His finger was over a button. "I created it as a parking thing, if we needed to narrow the car up a bit to get in a small space. But I guess we could use it here."

He turned round to Jack and Janet. "Um . . . it might get a bit cramped back there when I do this . . ."

Jack and Janet frowned. Rahul pressed the button. The car made a kind of grinding noise. And then the chassis began to move, expanding forwards and backwards, but getting, as it did so, thinner.

"Argh! What's happening?" said Janet.

"Crushed!" shouted Jack. "I'm getting crushed by the inside of this car! I DON'T WANT TO DIE!"

"You're not going to die!" said Rahul. Which was correct. The internal movement of the car stopped, leaving it less like a square, and more like a diamond, with Amy at the front and everyone else sitting behind her. The steering wheel had changed too – two tubular handles had popped out of the sides of it. The whole thing now looked more like . . .

"A motorbike . . . you've made it into a kind of motorbike!" said Amy.

Rahul looked pleased. He pointed at the button, which had a drawing on it of a motorbike.

"That's amazing," said Jack.

"Thank you. By the way, Jack . . . because you know I'm not very good at spotting it – when you were screaming, 'I DON'T WANT TO DIE!' – was that you being sarcastic?"

"Oh yes, Rahul," said Amy, interrupting, and seeing Jack go a bit red, "I'm sure it was."

Jack gave her a small smile.

She smiled back.

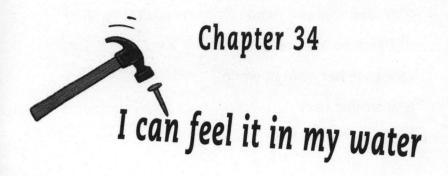

Chapter 34

I can feel it in my water

Meanwhile, the traffic jam had continued to stand still.

Amy looked at the new handles.

"What do I do?" she said. "Driving-wise, I mean."

Rahul shrugged. "It's just changed the shape a bit. So more or less what you've been doing."

"But more dodgy-inny-outy with the cars in front," said Janet.

"'Dodgy-inny-outy'?" said Jack. "Is that a thing?"

Amy gripped the direction lever.

"We're about to find out!"

She pushed the lever. The Taylor TurboChaser shot forward. Amy swerved it to the right. Cars and trucks were stuck all over the road, so it wasn't easy for her to understand which direction to head for.

Not only that, but all the other drivers – in the way that drivers do when they're in traffic jams – were constantly moving their vehicles about, trying to gain small little bits of ground.

Plus there were cars coming the other way.

So, once again, Amy slalomed.

"INNY!" shouted Janet, as Amy went to the inside of the lorry in front.

"OUTY!" shouted Janet, joined by Rahul, as Amy swerved back across the bus in front of the lorry.

"INNY!" shouted Janet and Rahul, as Amy went left again, and this time Jack, with a face and voice that said "I'm doing this sarcastically", joined in.

"DODGY!" shouted Janet and Rahul and Jack, as Amy's weaving in and out of the traffic continued.

Within a few minutes, Amy was at the front of the traffic queue. She looked round. To her side sat an old man and an old woman in one of those cars that have a normal car front and a wooden back. There were indeed some roadworks that were causing the jam. A not-very-proper-looking set of traffic lights sat in front of them, where nobody was working.

"Hello!" said the old man. He had on a flat cap. "You seem a little young to be out driving on this fine day, but perhaps it's just my eyes."

"They aren't what they were, are they, Mr Hancock?" said the old woman.

"Ooh! Who said that?" said the old man, looking round.

"Ha ha! Very good, Mr Hancock. You're as funny as you ever were!"

"Ha ha! Many thanks, Mrs Hancock."

Amy smiled back at them.

"What a lovely smile, Mr Hancock . . ."

"I agree, Mrs Hancock."

"What kind of car is this, young lady with the lovely smile?"

"He built it," said Amy, pointing at Rahul, who was blushing. "From my wheelchair."

"Ha ha, we've got another joker here, Mr Hancock! Young lady says her car is a wheelchair."

"No, it really is," said Amy. "Actually the wheelchair is still in here. But Rahul . . . added to it."

"Golly," said Mr Hancock. "What an ingenious fellow."

"I agree, Mr H."

"Hey . . ." said Jack, who was looking behind them at the rest of the traffic jam. "I hate to break up the love-in with the married couple from *Up*, but . . ."

"What?" said Rahul.

"Can I borrow the Binocuscope?"

"Yes," said Rahul, handing it over. Jack put it up to his eyes and looked out of the back of the TurboChaser.

"OK . . . I'm pretty sure . . . that's Mum's van."

"Where?" said Amy.

"At the back of the traffic jam!"

"Oh my days . . ." said Janet.

"Oh look, Mrs Hancock," said the old man. "I think the traffic lights are finally about to change. I can feel it in my water."

"Your water's never wrong, Mr Hancock."

Amy looked over at the old couple. "Excuse me," she said. "Could you do us a small favour?"

Chapter 35

Don't get cross

"They're near here, Suzi. I'm sure of it."

It was Prisha speaking.

"Yes, well," said Sanjay. "We were able to track them on Janet's phone for quite some time. But now I can't see it on my map."

"I think . . ." said Suzi, screwing up her eyes, ". . . that might be it? Right at the front, is it? Next to that Morris Minor Estate?"

Prisha, Sanjay, Colin and Norma all leant towards the front of the van to see.

"It looks a bit . . . thinner . . ." said Prisha. "And more like a . . . motorbike, than the photograph you showed us."

"Perhaps it's lost a bit of weight!" said Norma. "You should take a leaf out of its book, Colin!"

"I should. Hey! Perhaps I should go on a . . . Low-Car Diet!"

"HA HA HA HA!"

"I really hope we catch up with them soon," sighed Sanjay.

"But do you think that's them?" said Prisha. "That's the . . . Taylor TurboChaser?"

Sanjay looked out. "It might be."

"But . . . the thinness?"

"Yes. Thing is, Prisha . . . now don't get cross, darling . . ."

"It's never good when you say that, Sanjay."

"I know. But . . . don't get cross, darling . . ."

"WHAT IS IT?"

"I helped Rahul to build it, the TurboChaser . . . and . . ."

Suzi and Prisha looked at him.

"Go on . . ." said Prisha, eyes narrowing.

"Now, as I said, don't get cross, darling."

"GO ON!"

Sanjay started speaking very fast. "And we worked and worked on it so as to make it really really fast but we also built in lots of gadgets and tricks including the ability to shift its shape and loads of other things we may have got a bit carried away I'm sorry I should have told you earlier please don't get cross darling."

Prisha looked at him. She took a deep breath. She smiled.

"Of course not, darling."

"Thank you."

Then she hit him across the top of the head with her handbag.

"OW!"

"You stupid idiot! You great big fool!" She swung her handbag once more.

"OW! AGAIN!"

"Never happy being a wholesaler, were you, you always thought you should have been an inventor! And you've passed that on to our son! And for what? Just to make the job of catching him when he runs away in this stupid jalopy that much more difficult!"

She tried to hit him again. But this time he ducked.

"OW!"

"Sorry, Colin!" said Prisha.

"HA HA HA HA HA!"

"Stop laughing, Norma, that actually really hurt!"

"Shut up, everybody!" said Suzi. "We're moving!

The lights have changed! It's all fine, because I'm sure we'll catch up with them soon. We know they're not far away."

"Yes, of course," said Prisha, regaining her composure.

"Thank you, Suzi," said Sanjay, cowering.

"HA HA HA HA!"

"No, really, it still stings!"

There was then a pause of about thirty seconds when everyone in the car looked out, expecting the chase to begin in earnest.

"When you say . . . 'soon', Suzi," said Prisha, "doesn't *our* car have to move a bit for that to happen?"

"Yes. Well. I suppose a big traffic jam like this . . . once it starts to move, it takes a while to reach the back . . ."

"Yes. But I'm not sure it's moving *at all.*"

HONK! HONK! BEEP! HONK!

went the traffic.

Because Prisha was correct. The traffic jam was not moving. *At all*.

Chapter 36

A secret plan

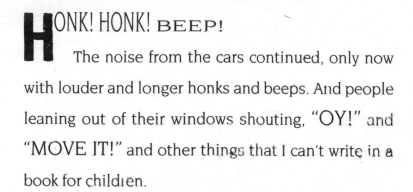

HONK! HONK! BEEP!

The noise from the cars continued, only now with louder and longer honks and beeps. And people leaning out of their windows shouting, "OY!" and "MOVE IT!" and other things that I can't write in a book for children.

"Thank you so much!" said Amy through the cat flap window of the TurboChaser. Not to the people swearing – that would be odd – but to Mr and Mrs Hancock.

Who were sitting in their car at the front of the traffic jam, very much *not* moving, despite the lights having turned to green.

"Pleasure!" said Mr Hancock.

"The people behind are going to be cross . . . !"

"Oh, don't worry about that! I'm deaf, aren't I, Mrs Hancock?"

"As a post, Mr Hancock."

Amy frowned. "How can you hear what I'm—"

"Lipreading. Best in the business, Mr Hancock is."

"Thanks for the compliments, as ever, Mrs H! Now, don't worry. I'm an old person, you see . . . more importantly, an old *driver* . . ."

"You're only as young as you feel, Mr H!"

"A truer word was never spoke, Mrs H! But my point is, these folk behind will see an old man at the wheel and just assume we never go over ten miles per hour. They'll still be cross, but they won't think it's all part of a –" he tapped his nose – "secret plan."

"Thank you again!" said Amy.

HONK! BEEP! HONK!

"DRIVE, YOU DECREPIT OLD IDIOT!"

"I think you'd best be off, my dear," said Mrs Hancock to Amy. "Particularly if you don't want to hear some words not suitable for children."

"Bye!" said Amy, and she let go of the direction lever.

"Send them our best at the Crazy Car Rally!" shouted Mr Hancock.

The TurboChaser, still in motorbike shape, shot forward and then round the corner, leaving Great Little Piddlington behind.

Meanwhile, at the back of the traffic jam, Suzi said: "Hmm."

Prisha said, "Ugh."

Sanjay said, "Sorry."

Colin said, "I can't believe it *still* hurts."

And Norma said, "HA HA HA HA HA!"

Chapter 37

As Simon Cowell says

"**W**ow . . ." said Janet. "That was nice of Mr and Mrs Hancock."

"One of the good things about being disabled, Janet," said Amy. "People are nice to you." She paused. "Well. Sometimes, anyway. Sometimes people are pretty horrible. But nice people are nice to you."

"*Nice people are nice to you,*" said Jack, in his teenager voice.

"Which obviously rules out *you*, of course."

Rahul turned the button that had changed the TurboChaser into its motorbike shape back the other way.

"AAAARGGGH!" said Janet. "The car is moving weirdly! Inside!"

"No, do you remember, Janet? This just happened."

"But it was the other way round. AAAA-RRGHH!"

"Yes, I'm just changing it back."

"Oh, OK," she said, suddenly calming down.

They drove for some time, leaving the traffic jam far behind. The countryside changed. They started driving through some very pretty places, with a lot of lakes everywhere.

For a while, there were no problems outside – no roadblocks, no diversions, no one in sight chasing them. But there were some problems inside.

"What's that smell?" said Amy, sniffing suddenly. "Is it the car?"

"No," said Rahul, "it's not the car. Nothing I put in this car could smell like that."

"Is it the countryside? Sometimes the countryside smells a bit like that."

"I don't think cows ever get *that* ill," said Janet.

"Jack . . ."

"What?"

"It's you, isn't it?"

"No."

"Come on," said Janet. "It is. I'm sure."

"Why are you so sure?"

"Because I've got a teenage brother too. And that is *definitely* the smell of teenage fart. Of teenage male fart." As she said this, Janet pushed her face – or at least her mouth and nose – out through the cat flap.

"Yes," said Amy. "It is."

"I think so too," said Rahul. "And I don't even have a teenage brother. But I have a *lot* of cousins. And we meet and eat a *lot* of Indian food . . ."

"All right, all right!" said Jack. "Yes! OK! I've let off! I'm sure some of *you* have during this journey as well!"

"Oh my goodness, yes," said Amy.

"As Simon Cowell says, 'It's a yes from me,'" said Janet, bringing her face back inside.

"Um . . . well, if we're all admitting it, then, yes, I too have broken wind," said Rahul. "Once or twice."

"But . . ." said Amy, "we aren't teenagers. So our farts don't smell as bad."

"Is it time to stop for some lunch?" said Janet.

"Smell not put you off then, Jan?" said Jack.

"It's gone away now."

"Hmm. Maybe we could stop," said Amy. "We've probably put enough distance between us and Mum's van. We're nearly in Cumbria, I think. And we have –" she looked at the clock – "over twenty-four hours before Dad leaves for Japan. What have we got to eat?"

Janet took out her bag. "Beans!"

Everyone looked at Jack.

"I think it might be time to see if we can get some different food," he said.

Chapter 38

Chill out, sis

"Hmmmm. I loved that chocolate ice cream!"

"It was delicious. Although not as nice as the apple crumble!"

"The jelly trifle was incredible!"

"I liked the main course – roast chicken and roast potatoes!"

"So, Jack, shall we get the hill?" said Amy.

The children were sitting round a white-table-clothed table, having stopped at La Rurale Pastorale, an extremely posh restaurant in an old country house just outside Dermot Coillery (the place names in this part of the country sounded more like famous people than rude things; they had passed the villages of Bear Hills, Dredd Sheeran, Huge Bonne Ville and Vince Cable).

Waiters with very noticeable French accents and white silk gloves had served them an amazing repast, with drinks and puddings and lots of side dishes. And they'd stopped here, on the basis not only that Jack shouldn't be given any more beans, but also that he had said that eating at La Rurale Pastorale would not be a problem, money-wise. He, as the oldest person on board the TurboChaser – virtually an adult, really – would sort it.

"The bill?" Jack replied, to Amy. "I don't think there's much point in asking for that."

"I beg your pardon?"

"I thought you had some money," said Janet.

"I never said that."

"You said that eating here wouldn't be a problem!" said Rahul.

"That I did!"

"So, Jack," said Amy, "what did you mean?"

"I think you're forgetting that Jack is short for . . . Jack the Lad."

"Is it?" said Janet.

"Well, no," said Jack. "Not technically. But what I mean is, I'm a trickster. I'm a master of the short, and the long, con. I'm the man with a plan. And I have one."

"Oh good," said Rahul.

Jack frowned. "That sounded a bit . . . sarcastic."

"Might be. I think I'm starting to learn how to do it."

"We can't just . . . not pay," said Janet. "It's not right."

"And she's not wrong," said Rahul. "For once."

"Jack . . ." said Amy. "I don't like this."

"Don't worry," said Jack, smiling. "You'll see." He beckoned over their waiter, a man with a large moustache. The waiter bent down towards him.

"'Allo, zir. Ah trust you 'ave enjoyed your me-al?"

"Yes, thank you. It was delicious."

"I 'ave ze bill 'ere," he said, presenting a little silver platter with a dome. He lifted the dome, and there it was – £127.50.

"Oh my days," said Janet.

"I wish I'd looked at the prices now," said Rahul.

"Is zere a problem, zir?" said the waiter.

"No, no," said Jack. "What's your name?"

"Mah naime?"

"No, your *name*."

"Mah naime?"

"Oh, you're saying 'name'. Yes."

The waiter seemed to think about this for quite some time. "Louis."

"OK, Louis. Well. If I could be frank. We can't pay that. We can't pay anything like that. I mean they're children, aren't they? And I'm only fourteen. So we don't have jobs. So, like, no money."

Louis's moustache seemed to twitch.

"Zis is a joke, yes? 'Ilarious Breeteesh sense of 'umour – ha ha ha ha."

"No. No. Now, I can see you're getting annoyed. Your moustache is twitching."

Louis frowned. He put his hand up to it to check.

"But I think you're forgetting something, aren't you?" Jack added.

"Ah am?"

"You are. My sister – over there – I think you're forgetting – she's in a wheelchair." Jack started to look very sad. His eyes moistened. "And I can't believe that this wonderful establishment – La Rurale Pastorale – is going to force a disabled young girl and her brother, and all her friends, who are just trying to help her live her tiny, difficult, problem-filled life from day to day, to sing for their suppers? I mean, really?"

Louis's moustache twitched again. He frowned. He frowned some more.

"Would you maaained just waitin' a *minute*, please? Ah need to 'ave a word wiz mah *superioeours*."

"Of course," said Jack. "You take your time."

Louis nodded, turned on his heel and went off. Jack turned to the table, smiled, and opened his palms, in a "You see? Sorted!" kind of way.

"Me?" hissed Amy furiously. "*I'm* your big *clever* plan?"

"Yes. Sorry about that. I had to lay it on a bit thick."

"My tiny, difficult, problem-filled life? I love my life! And you *know* that one thing I *never* do is use my legs as an excuse! When anyone asks for volunteers to do something, I *never* stick my hand up and say 'I can't! I'm disabled!'"

"As I say, I had to turn on the waterworks a bit. Chill out, sis."

"Why are you speaking like a middle-aged DJ?"

"All I'm saying is, you'll thank me when they come back and let us off. You will." He looked round. Louis was returning. "As they are *definitely* about to do . . ."

Chapter 39

Definitely sarcastically

"**H**ow much more washing-up is there to do?" said Jack.

"Loads," said Louis. "As you can see."

Except it now turned out his name wasn't Louis. It was Dave. And he didn't have a French accent any more. He had a *very* British accent, located somewhere in the middle of the country. He was standing with his arms crossed by the sink, in the back of La Rurale Pastorale's kitchen. As he spoke,

a whole new load of plates, knives, forks, pots and pans were emptied into the very same sink. By Rahul.

"Oh, come on!" said Jack. "We've been here for three hours!"

Amy, Janet and Rahul looked at him. Amy was on drying duties; Janet on stacking-up duties; and Rahul, as I've basically already told you, was on bringing-new-needing-to-be-washed-up-cutlery-and-crockery-over-to-the-sink duties.

Dave checked his watch. "And I reckon

you'll be here for *another* two hours. And then maybe you'll have paid your bill. Just about. You stupid little boy."

He started to walk off, grabbing a piece of expensive bread from the counter to chew as he went.

"What now, Jack the Lad?" said Amy, flicking him with her tea towel. The restaurant had provided her with a chair, which she was sitting on while she dried the dishes.

"Yeah, what now, Mr Short and Long Con?" said Janet.

"You did really well there, Jack, I must say," said Rahul.

"Hmm," said Amy. "You *have* learnt how to be sarcastic."

Jack turned wildly away from the sink, towards Dave's walking-away back.

"I'll tell everyone the French thing is a big act!"

shouted Jack. "I'll tell everyone . . . everyone . . . who follows me on my Instagram page!"

"Yeah," shouted Dave back. "You do that, Katy Perry." And he walked out of the kitchen.

By the time they left La Rurale Pastorale – with Dave waving them off, *definitely* sarcastically (he was holding in his waving hand a very, very clean plate, for a start) – and got back into the Taylor TurboChaser, it was getting dark.

"OK," said Amy, as they drove away. "I think it's beans from now on. I don't care about the smell."

Chapter 40

HOT ROD

No one said anything for a while. Amy just drove.

"Well . . ." said Rahul, eventually. "I guess we lost a lot of time there."

"You think?" said Jack.

"Yes, I do. And yes, I know you're being sarcastic."

"Estimated arrival time at destination 23:30pm, Saturday," said the sat nav.

"Yes, we're cutting it a bit fine now," said Amy.

"Thanks a lot, Jack."

This time, Jack didn't say anything. Not even sarcastically.

"Do you think our parents are somewhere nearby?" said Janet, looking around.

"I don't know," said Amy. "I suppose so."

The mood in the car had become very depressed.

Janet said, "Can I turn my phone on, then?"

Amy looked at Rahul. "Probably won't make much difference now. They'll probably catch up with us any second."

Rahul nodded.

Janet picked up her phone.

"*Aaaaaaaah* . . ." she said.

"Why are you making that noise?" said Amy. "That's like the sound my mum makes when she's gone on about how much she's gasping for a cup of tea and then makes a cup of tea and drinks the first gulp."

"Because that's how I feel!" said Janet, with her phone held up in her hand. "I'm gasping to turn my phone on!"

"Hold on, Janet!" said Rahul suddenly.

"Oh no!" said Janet. "What?"

"That car up ahead . . ."

"I've turned it on! I couldn't help myself!"

"Well, turn it off!" said Rahul.

"What about the car up ahead?" said Amy.

"It's not a car, is it? It's a van."

Amy squinted at it.

"It's a van . . . with quite a high top on it."

Now Jack squinted at it.

"And –" he got out the Binocuscope and peered through it – "a sticker on the back that says 'HOT ROD'."

"Oh my days," said Amy. "Our parents aren't about to catch *up* with us. They're ahead of us! *We've* caught up with *them*!"

"Janet!" shouted Rahul. *"Have you turned your phone off?"*

"Er . . ."

"JANET!" they all cried.

Chapter 41

Like when you run at some sheep

"**T**his is a *really* narrow lane for the van," said Suzi. "If a car comes the other way, I'll just have to reverse back down it."

"Ooh, hello," said Norma, looking at her phone. "I've got a blinking dot on my maps!"

"You can get some powder for that, y'know!" said Colin.

"HA HA HA HA HA!" he and Norma said together.

"Sorry, what?" said Prisha.

"I said that black spot on my app is winking again!" said Norma.

"We'd better call the doctor, then!" said Colin.

"HA HA HA HA HA!"

"Yes, that's basically the same joke, Colin," said Sanjay.

"But more importantly, *where* are you seeing that dot?"

Norma held up her phone. Sanjay squinted at it.

"Well?" said Suzi, because she couldn't look  round at it while she was driving. "How far in front of us are they?"

"Um…well, given that the world is round, a long, long way," said Sanjay.

"Pardon?"

"They aren't in front

of us. They're behind us." He looked round. "In fact, I can *see* them."

"WHAT?" said Suzi, and she looked in the mirror. "That's them?"

"Yes! I recognise my own power torches!"

"They're chasing *us* now? Why?" said Colin.

"They're not chasing us, you fool!" said Norma. "It's like when you run at some sheep. If you catch up with the sheep and then run ahead of them, the stupid sheep will keep running after you because they can't remember what they're running away from!"

"Oh yes. Didn't Janet's friend Malcolm Bailey talk about that once?"

Suzi screeched to a halt. "Right," she said. "They're not getting away this time."

Chapter 42

Calm as a cucumber

"**A**AAARGH!" said the passengers of the Taylor TurboChaser as *they* screeched to a halt as well, about twenty metres behind the parent-filled van.

"They've stopped!" said Rahul.

"The van doors are opening!" said Janet.

"They're getting out!" said Jack.

"Hold on!" said Amy, looking over her shoulder and pulling the direction lever backwards towards her. The TurboChaser went into reverse, making a loud groaning sound as it did so.

Suzi and the other parents just stood and watched, amazed. From the point of view of the children looking out from the Taylor TurboChaser, the adults got smaller and smaller. Not small enough, however, for Rahul not to notice what they were doing.

"They're getting back into the van!" he shouted.

"OK!" shouted Amy. "I'll keep reversing!"

"You better had!" shouted Rahul. "Because now *they're* reversing!"

They were. Amy's face – looking over her shoulder – set itself now into a determined expression. The backwards car chase was on!

"Why have you put your wings on again, Janet?" Amy screamed.

"They're clean and dry again!"

"Please take them off! I can't see out the back!"

The narrow lane curved round. Amy moved the wheel to turn the TurboChaser. But it started heading instead towards the hedge running by the roadside!

"Other way, Amy! You have to turn the wheel the opposite way when you reverse!"

"Oh yes! Yes!" She did so, bringing the back of the vehicle in line with the lane just in time. Leaves brushed against the glass next to Janet's head as it swung round.

The van, or rather the back of it, was getting closer.

"Come on, Amy!" said Rahul.

"Yeah, come on, Amy!" said Jack.

"Was that sarcastic?" said Rahul.

"No!" said Jack.

"I don't know if I can make it go any faster!" said Amy. "It doesn't like going backwards very much!"

"Neither do I!" shouted Janet. "It's making me feel sick!"

"Fox!" shouted Jack.

"Don't be rude!" shouted Amy.

"No! In the road! Behind us!"

Sitting there, calm as a cucumber – calmer in some ways, as a cucumber would definitely have been about to be squashed – was indeed a russet-brown fox.

"OH!" Quick as a flash, Rahul pressed the motorbike button and the TurboChaser narrowed.

Quicker even than that quick flash, Amy swerved the handlebars.

The TurboChaser circled round the fox at the last minute. It – the TurboChaser, not the fox – groaned terribly as it went.

"Is it going to fall apart, Rahul?"

"I don't know!"

"Hang on!" said Janet. "Look!"

They looked. The van had stopped reversing. It was just standing in the lane, waiting.

"Why is it doing that?" said Amy.

"It's the fox!"

It *was* the fox. Which clearly was a *very* calm fox, given that, despite a backwards car chase going on around it, it had settled down to sleep, for all the world like a cat in a basket.

"Aah! Good old Mum!" said Jack.

"What do you mean?" said Janet.

"He means our mum would never run over an animal," said Amy, and she felt strangely proud of Suzi – even though she was running away from her.

They continued to reverse away. The van receded into the distance. The lane was still narrow, but now on either side of it were two enormous lakes. Very enormous lakes. Amy couldn't even see the other sides of them.

"Yay!" shouted Janet. "Way to go, Amy!"

"Whoa!" shouted Rahul. "Another victory for the Taylor TurboChaser!"

"Hurray!" shouted Jack in the same tone. "And now there's a police car behind us!"

Amy stopped reversing. They all looked round.

There was.

"*Stop right there,*" said an official-sounding voice over a megaphone.

Chapter 43

The Eagle and the Squirrel

"**R**oger. The Eagle has taken roost. I repeat, the Eagle has taken roost. The Squirrel is in the Eagle's sights. The Eagle is poised to dive. Over."

"Sorry, PC Middleton, what are you saying?"

DCI Bryant was in the driving seat. PC Middleton was in the passenger seat. They were both looking out at the back of the Taylor TurboChaser.

"Sorry, sir, is it not clear?" said PC Middleton.

"Basically, the Eagle is us. This car. And the Squirrel is them – the kids – in that weird vehicle. And so when I say, 'The Squirrel is in the Eagle's sights,' what I mean is—"

"I KNOW WHAT YOU MEAN!" shouted DCI Bryant. "I JUST DON'T KNOW WHY YOU'RE SPEAKING LIKE THAT! YOU'RE NOT EVEN ON A WALKIE-TALKIE! YOU'RE ON THE PHONE TO MRS TAYLOR!"

PC Middleton nodded, as he often did when DCI Bryant lost his temper. He was indeed on the phone to Suzi, who had got out of the van, with the other parents.

"*Yes,*" her voice was saying from the little speaker on PC Middleton's phone. "*I didn't really understand why you were speaking like that either.*"

"Just felt right, madam."

"*OK. Well, thank you for getting here so quickly after my call telling you where we were . . .*"

"That was me, Mrs Taylor," said DCI Bryant. "I'm the one driving."

"Well, I'm not sure that matters."

DCI Bryant looked a little put out by this.

"The important thing," Suzi continued, "is that we've found them. And I don't think – finally – they can get away now."

She hung up the phone.

The two policemen got out of their car.

Amy's mum was right. The kids couldn't escape now.

Chapter 44

Please, no

"**W**ell. I think the game's up, everybody," said Amy, watching as the adults approached from both sides. "I guess you lot may as well get out and hand yourselves in. I'll stay in my chair. In the car . . ."

"Sorry, Amy!" said Jack loudly. "Sorry, everyone! I held us up for ages with that stupid plan at the restaurant. It's all my fault!"

"Yes," said Amy. "It is."

"Oh," said Jack, deflated. "I was hoping you might tell me it wasn't. Or that it didn't matter now. And I hadn't, after all, spoiled everything."

"Nope," said Amy.

"Hmm," said Jack. "Fair enough."

He started to lift up the handles on his side of the TurboChaser to get out. Janet started to do so on the other side. But then, suddenly, Rahul said, "Hold on."

"What?" said Amy.

"There's a gap in the hedge to your right . . ."

"OK . . ."

"Just wide enough to get through . . ."

"Yes . . ." said Amy. "I'm still waiting for you to notice that there's not a field there, like there was last time. Not even a field with cows and a bull. There's a *lake*. A really, really big lake."

"I know."

Amy stared at him. Jack and Janet held their places.

"Are you saying . . . ?"

"I'm not saying anything. Except, I've got an idea."

"Oh no," said Janet. "Please, no."

Chapter 45

Sorry, Mum!

The police remained on one side of the TurboChaser and the parents on the other. DCI Bryant took out a hand-held megaphone.

"Er . . . I think it might be best," said Suzi, "if I speak to my daughter."

DCI Bryant frowned, and held up his palm to her. "Please stand back, Mrs Taylor. We have a police policy in these circumstances."

"Yes," said PC Middleton, "I think *we* know how to

handle this, thank you very much. We are the police, after all."

Suzi looked at Prisha, who shrugged. DCI Bryant brought the megaphone to his lips.

"STEP OUT OF THE CAR. STEP OUT OF THE CAR. TURN OFF THE ENGINE AND STEP OUT OF THE CAR. WITH YOUR HANDS UP."

"With your hands up?" said Prisha. "What are you talking about?"

"They might have guns!" said PC Middleton.

"Of course they haven't got guns!" said Suzi.

DCI Bryant thought about it for a second. Then he put the megaphone up to his mouth.

"OK. JUST STEP OUT OF THE CAR. YOU CAN PUT YOUR HANDS . . . WHEREVER."

Nothing happened. The adults looked at each other.

"Are you *sure* I shouldn't do the speaking?" said Suzi again. "I mean, I don't know if we need a megaphone. I can just go and tap on the window and—"

"Oh, for heaven's sake," said Prisha, coming forward and banging on the glass. "Rahul! Rahul! Just get out of there!"

"Yes! And Janet! Come on!" shouted Colin.

"Yes! Come on, Janet!" shouted Norma.

"Er . . . everybody . . ." said Suzi. "I don't think screaming at them is a great idea."

Suzi was right about that. Because inside the

car, Amy looked out at the contorted faces of the shouting parents, and a thought came into her head. *Trust your instincts, they'll never betray you.* One of her mum's quotes again! But it helped her make a decision.

"Sorry, Mum!" she shouted from inside the car. "But in a way it's your fault!"

She turned the wheel to the right, and threw the direction lever forward.

Chapter 46

Does it still work if it gets wet?

The Taylor TurboChaser moved off towards the right, towards the gap in the hedge and the very large lake beyond.

"What! Wait? What is she doing?" said Suzi.

"The how, the what, the why is going on now?" said Colin.

"Stop!" said Prisha.

"YES! STOP WHAT YOU'RE DOING!" said DCI Bryant through the megaphone. "TURN OFF THE

CAR! THERE'S A LAKE OVER THERE! YOU CAN'T GO THAT WAY!"

To try to drown him out, Amy turned on the sat nav. Which unfortunately said, "THERE'S A LAKE OVER THERE! YOU CAN'T GO THAT WAY!"

She turned it off. The car continued on its way through the hedge.

"TURN THE ENGINE OFF AND STEP AWAY FROM THE CAR!" said DCI Bryant.

"That's not helping! Shut up!" said Prisha.

"Please, Amy!" screamed Suzi. "Don't drive into the water!"

Inside the car, Jack was feeling much the same way as his mum.

"Hello? Water? Immediately in front of us? Deep water? I know this car is partly made out of fish tanks, but last time I looked none of us are actually fish?"

"I trust Rahul!" shouted Amy. "He hasn't let us down yet!"

"No, but I'm worried he's going to let us down now – far down – into the deep!"

"I can't swim!" said Janet.

"Really?" said Rahul. "What about your wings?"

"What?"

"They're not water ones?"

"No, they're fairy ones!"

"You can swim, Janet," said Amy. "I've seen you in the local pool."

"OK, but I thought I'd shout it anyway, just to try and stop you!"

The adults were all running behind, through the gap in the hedge, shouting and screaming at Amy to stop. The wheels of the TurboChaser were now on the small bank of grass at the edge of the lake.

"Are you sure about this?" whispered Amy.

"No," said Rahul.

"Great," said Amy, and she carried on driving forward. With a huge splash, the Taylor TurboChaser entered the water. At this point, it was quite shallow. But Amy figured it would get deep pretty quickly. The lake was huge, and surrounded by hills that turned into mountains in the distance.

Rahul pressed the button to raise up the chassis and make it into a four-by-four. This, at least, took the body of the car out of the water.

"Keep going!" said Rahul, climbing out of his cat flap.

"What do you mean, keep going! You're leaving?"

"I'm not!" He climbed on to the front of the TurboChaser. "I'm staying with you, Amy! All the way to Scotland!"

"No, don't keep going! Let's give up!" said Janet. "My mum's waving some biscuits!"

She was. Norma had waded knee-deep into the water and was waving a packet of chocolate digestives at the back of the car, as if she was using the packet like a flag, like those people in airports

do who direct aeroplanes. Unfortunately, every time the packet waved towards Colin, he took one.

"Ooh!" said Jack. "I'm tempted too. Turn back! Before her dad eats them all!"

"We're not turning back for a biscuit!" shouted Amy, glancing in the rear-view mirror. The two policemen were wading into the lake, followed by the parents. Suzi, who was not a tall woman, was already up to her chest.

DCI Bryant still had the megaphone.

"COME BACK! COME BACK! YOU WILL DROWN!"

"I'm worried about the megaphone, sir!" said PC Middleton. "Does it still work if it gets wet?"

"OF COURSE IT . . . *fizzzzz* . . . *ccchhhh* . . . does."

DCI Bryant moved the device away from his mouth and turned it upside down. It made a dying, buzzing noise. "Oh."

Amy looked at Rahul, balanced on the bonnet in front of her. "How much further can this go?" she shouted. Water was starting to lap at the sides of the car windows.

"Just need . . . a bit . . . more . . ." shouted Rahul back.

She moved further forward, but the car made the loudest groaning noise it had made so far. It sounded like a large, wild creature in pain. Outside, on the glass, the water rose again.

"AAARRGGH!" screamed Janet. "WATER! IT'S COMING IN THROUGH THE CAT FLAPS!"

"YEAH! IT IS!" shouted Jack.

"Rahul . . ." said Amy, "we can't go on—"

"Now!" said Rahul, and he dived down into the water.

Chapter 47

Exactly the opposite

"**O**h no!" screamed Prisha. "Oh no! Sanjay! Swim out! Save our child!"

"Our child can swim, Prisha. You know that. We paid for him to have extra lessons!"

"You should swim out and save him anyway!"

But while they were arguing, Rahul had emerged from the water – which wasn't that deep where he was, anyway, so he could still stand – and had bent down by the car and put his arm into the water. He was turning something – the crank on the front of the bonnet, near the TAYTURB1 number plate. The one that turned the Taylor TurboChaser into a tent.

"Press the teepee button, Amy!" he shouted.

Amy did as he instructed. The parents and the police stared, baffled, as suddenly reams of Joseph-and-his-Amazing-Technicolor-Dreamcoat-style material came flood-ing out of the chimney in the middle of the vehicle. And indeed you might be baffled, too, as to what Rahul was doing.

But – if you remember – making the car into a tent also spread the underside of the TurboChaser out, and the underside of the TurboChaser was lined with . . . air-filled mattresses. So suddenly the Taylor TurboChaser was floating! The sheer momentum of the heavy vehicle caused it to carry on, further into the lake.

"Ha! That's amazing!" said Amy.

"It's a boat!" shouted Jack.

"It's a ferry!" shouted Janet.

"It's — " said Rahul, climbing back through the cat flap " – the Taylor Turbo-Dinghy!"

"One problem . . ." said Amy. "We *are* floating.

Well done. But we're not moving. And –" she looked round – "I think the police and our parents might be deciding to come after us."

DCI Bryant and PC Middleton were, indeed, back on the shore, putting on waterproofs and galoshes and big plastic knee-length waders. PC Middleton was having a lot of trouble doing this and had ended up on the ground on his bottom with his legs in the air, while Colin and Norma tried to wedge the waders on to his feet.

"Push, Norma! Push, Colin!"

"We're pushing!"

"Get on with it, Middleton!"

"I told the Police Store I was an eight and a half, sir. These are definitely eights!"

Suzi, meanwhile, wasn't bothering with waders. Amy watched as her mum simply peeled off her jacket and dived into the water, and then began to swim.

Amy felt a pang of guilt about that, but she had to get to Scotland. So she just turned to Rahul and said, "We need to go faster!"

Her mum had settled into a front crawl and was

moving quickly into the lake after them.

"OK," said Rahul. "I have an idea for that too. For how to move the car. Press the hazards!"

"The hazards?"

"Yes!"

Amy pressed the button. The red flag popped out of the back left-hand side of the car.

"OK – there's a second button next to it. Press that one too."

She did so. A second red flag popped out of the back right-hand side of the car. So now there were two big flags flapping in the wind at the back of the car.

"What . . . are they doing?" said PC Middleton, in the shallow water on the edge of the lake. "Are they telling us they're in trouble?"

"Right," said Rahul. "Jack, Janet – stick your hands out of the cat flaps and grab the bottom end of the flags." They did so. "Got them?"

"Yes," said Jack.

"Yes," said Janet.

"OK. Now pull them tight!"

They did. The flags stopped flapping and became taut. And, as that happened, the Taylor Turbo-Dinghy started to move. Fast.

"The flags . . . they've become sails!" said Amy.

"Yes," said Rahul.

"You're a genius, Rahul!" said Jack.

"Now I know you're being sarcastic!"

"I'm definitely not!" said Jack, laughing.

Rahul hit the radio. *"We are sailing . . ."* came a song blasting from the speakers.

"Although, how long do we have to hold on to these?" said Janet. "My hands are freezing."

They swept across the lake in the Turbo-Dinghy. Suzi, still swimming after them, dwindled into tininess, as they left her behind. Soon, she stopped swimming, and turned back to shore.

In the shallows, watching the children sail away into the distance, Prisha looked at PC Middleton and said, "In answer to your question, no, I don't think they're telling us they're in trouble. In fact, I think exactly the opposite."

Chapter 48

A nice-looking restaurant

"**O**h well," said Suzi, "at least we know where they're headed."

"Well, not exactly," said Prisha. "It's huge that lake – we've no idea which bit of the shore they might land on."

"What about sending out a boat?" said Norma, to DCI Bryant.

"*Boaty McBoatface*, you mean?" said Colin.

"Shh, Colin," said Norma.

"You're no fun any more," said Colin sulkily.

"We've radioed for it, Mrs Warner, but I'm afraid there are no police boats available, unless it's an emergency."

"It *is* an emergency!"

"Not if their craft is not sinking, apparently. Which last time I saw it, it very much wasn't."

"No, but I mean . . ." said Suzi, ". . . at least we know where they're going. In general. Because once they're across that lake, it's only a few miles to Scotland."

"So you think," said Sanjay, "they're definitely, definitely trying to get to Amy's dad?"

Suzi paused. She had changed out of her wet clothes into some trousers and a jumper provided by Colin, who "in case of accidents" – something Suzi didn't want to think about – always travelled with a spare pair. They were much too big for her, and the cuffs of his jumper kept falling into the food she was trying to eat.

Because the parents and police – who themselves were hungry and tired – had decided to discuss what to do over dinner, so had turned round and driven back to a nice-looking restaurant they'd passed earlier.

"Yes. I mean . . . he's the one who paid for the new wheelchair."

"Isn't he also the one," said Prisha, "who's furious because of what Rahul has *done* to the new wheelchair?"

"Yes. But I guess Amy thinks she can turn him round."

Prisha looked at her. "Is he the type of man who gets turned round?"

Suzi stared into her glass of water. She shook her head.

"*I'm* the type of man who gets turned round!"

said Colin, getting up and whizzing round in a circle, ending up facing Norma.

Norma shook her head. "Sorry, Colin. Not appropriate."

"Oh," said Colin.

"Amy . . ." continued Suzi, "she really loves her dad. Kind of idolises him. Thinks he's perfect."

"It's easier to seem perfect when you're not there," said Prisha, looking away.

"Yes," said Suzi. "I mean he IS a good dad. In some ways. But – well – the accident. The one that left Amy unable to walk. Peter – my husband – was driving. I mean . . . he didn't do anything wrong; it *was* an accident. But still, I think he blamed himself. And so he's never – I think – quite been able to accept Amy in a wheelchair."

Prisha nodded. Sanjay was quiet. Colin made a gesture that meant, "Shall I whizz round again?" Norma shook her head.

"Anyway. We split up soon afterwards. So, I don't know – it's bad enough that we're having to chase her and the others up and down the country. But I'm not even sure that her plan to change Peter's mind is going to work."

"Oh dear," said Prisha.

"Yes. And it gets worse. I spoke to him just now and he said – not pleased at all – that if we couldn't catch the kids, he was going to organise something else."

"What something else?" said Sanjay.

"I dunno. But it sounded ominous."

She put her glass down. No one said anything for a moment.

Then a voice said, "Madame, would you laaaike ze bill? Or is zere anyzing else we can get for you *aelle*?"

Everyone looked up. Louis was twiddling his moustache and smiling. Prisha said, "*Non, tout a été bien, merci. La facture serait super, mais juste un petit renseignement, s'il vous plaît: le service est-il inclus?"*

And Louis said, "Pardon?" But not in a French accent.

Chapter 49

Mobilcon XR-207. Located

A bump woke Amy up. Then another bump. She opened her eyes slowly.

Looking back at her were two very big brown eyes. Then they got further away. Then they came back again. Then they got further away again. At this point, as Amy's own vision cleared from sleep, the two very big brown eyes were joined by a twitching nose and two very big grey ears. As the sight started to get closer again, Amy shouted, "Hey! I think we've hit land. Somewhere near where the Teletubbies live!"

"Say what?" said Rahul sleepily.

"There's a huge rabbit outside!" said Amy. "So unless it's a rabbit fish, we must have got across the lake overnight!"

After they'd set off from the opposite shore, the movement of the TurboChaser had slowed down a lot. It was difficult for Jack and Janet to hold on to the flags for too long, so they'd kept on stopping to give their arms a rest.

Eventually, Rahul had found a way of pinning them to the outside of the cat flaps – the flags, that is, not Jack and Janet – so that they would continue to work as sails without the need for hands to hold them tight. But it was slow going, and night had begun to fall.

"What shall we do?" Amy had said, in between munching. They were drifting, and she couldn't really steer on the water, so the children had decided to have dinner. Beans, obviously.

"Well," said Rahul, looking around. The inside was all spread out, and they were protected by the tent material, so it felt quite cosy. "Although it is presently the Taylor Turbo-Dinghy, it is also the Taylor Turbo-Tent. So we could just sleep in it."

"On the lake?"

"Well, yes."

"Is it safe?" said Janet. "Sleeping on the lake?"

"Obviously not," said Jack. "But what *has* been so far, on this trip?"

They had all thought about this for a bit, and decided that, for once, Jack had said something sensible, and so, as soon as the beans had been eaten, they all went to bed. The slow movement of the waves on the lake rocked them all gently to sleep. Until the rabbit alarm-clock moment.

All the children woke up, excited to see the

rabbit. It was very early in the morning, and it was bright and cold on the edge of the lake, but there was something joyful and wonderful in having made it through another night, and then being woken up by an enormous rabbit. Which didn't even run away or anything, just looked at the children as they appeared, its nose twitching away.

"I'm not sure it's a rabbit," said Jack.

"Yes, it might be a hare," said Rahul.

"It's obviously not a hair," said Janet, holding up a strand of hers.

Amy smiled. She looked back over the lake. The sun was shining, and threads of light glittered on the surface of the water. She wondered, suddenly, if this was the lake where her dad had stopped, all those years ago, to take that family photo, the one where they had all been laughing. She was about to ask Jack whether he thought it was as well, when she remembered the more immediate fact that her dad was leaving for Japan in . . . she checked the clock. *Five hours.*

"I think, whether it's a rabbit or hare," she said, pressing the button to return the TurboChaser to its car shape, rather than its dinghy one, "it's a good-luck omen. Let's get going!"

"Return to the highlighted route," said the sat nav. "You are currently in a lake."

"You are currently in a lake," said Jack, evidently back to his usual self.

Amy drove up on to the shore, out of the lake and into a field. Then she turned towards a gate, beyond which it looked like there was a lane, leading north.

"Mobilcon. XR-207. Located," said a robotic voice, which sounded like it was coming from somewhere above them. **"Mobilcon. XR-207. Located,"**

The children looked at each other.

"What was that?" said Amy, frightened.

"Was it the rabbit?" said Janet. "Maybe it's rabbit-speak?"

"It came from . . . the sky," said Rahul.

They all looked up. To see, hovering about three metres above them, a black shining disc, powered by four tiny fans. Two small red lights on the front of it blinked at them, like devil's eyes.

"DRONE! DRONE!" shouted Jack. And they all dived for cover.

Chapter 50

The sort of thing they say in old films

"**Mobilcon. XR-207. Located,**" said the drone again.

Jack looked up. Amy – who had only been able to bend down in her seat – opened her eyes.

"Is that all it does?" she whispered.

"I dunno," said Rahul.

"I doubt it," said Jack.

"What's the Mubbel Cone XR-007?" said Janet.

"The wheelchair," said Rahul. "The one that's still actually at the heart of the TurboChaser."

"OK . . . well . . . maybe if we just drive quietly away . . ." said Amy. She pushed the direction lever forward gently.

"Mobilcon. XR-207. Moving," said the drone.

"Uh-oh," said Jack.

"I think it's seen what you're doing," said Janet.

"Right. Well, maybe I'll just carry on driving away, and let it do its commentary," said Amy. "I mean, what difference can that make?"

"Mobilcon. XR-207. Initiating override."

"I don't like the sound of that!" said Rahul.

"It's OK," said Amy, driving the TurboChaser up to a gate, and turning right to get on to the road—

"Oh," she said, as the TurboChaser came out of the gate and turned left. "It's not OK."

"Why?" said Rahul.

"I turned the other way! But the car isn't obeying."

"WHERE ARE WE GOING?" screamed Janet. "WHO'S CONTROLLING THE CAR?"

Amy frantically tried to pull the steering wheel back round. But it made no difference. The TurboChaser seemed hypnotised. They carried on driving the wrong way. Above and just in front of them, the drone flew on. It was like it was pulling them magnetically.

"Mobilcon. XR-207. Returning product to company," said the drone.

"Oh my days," said Jack. "This will be Dad's work!"

"Will it?" said Amy.

"Yes! He said he wanted to get the wheelchair returned, didn't he? He'll have got Mobilcon to send out this drone to—"

"Two hundred miles to destination."

"Two hundred miles!" said Amy.

"Back towards where we came from!" said Rahul.

"How is it doing this?" said Amy.

"I don't know!" said Rahul. "It must've put some kind of remote lock on the original wheelchair. And now it's controlling it!"

"And how do we stop it?"

"That I *really* don't know."

"Fabulous. Turns out you really are a great scientist, Rahul!" said Jack.

"Shut up, Jack," said Amy. "Rahul got us this far and he'll sort this out! Won't you, Rahul?"

"Umm . . ."

"One hundred and ninety-nine miles to destination."

No one said anything. The car carried on going. *Away* from Scotland. Amy shook her head. She sighed and was about to say, "I guess we may as well give up, then," when Janet said, "It sounds a bit like the sat nav."

They all turned to her.

"Don't you think?" She did an impression of the drone – *"One hundred and ninety-nine miles to destination."*

"Which sat nav voice do you mean?" said Amy. "The Welsh one, the shouty one, or the last, smooth-sounding one?"

"All of them."

"Right," said Jack. "Good thought. Useful."

"Actually," said Rahul. "It might be."

"How?"

"One hundred and ninety-eight miles to destination."

"Well . . . that drone is on an electromagnetic frequency. It's probably controlling the chair using radio waves. Which have a specific wavelength. That's how everything electronic works."

"OK," said Amy.

"So if the sat nav is on a similar frequency . . . I don't know – it might interfere with the drone. There's just a chance."

"It's a long shot," said Jack. "But it might just work."

"Is that sarcastic?" said Rahul.

"Yes. It's the sort of thing they say in old films."

"OK," said Rahul, turning round. "You got any better ideas, Mr Man with a Plan?"

Jack didn't answer.

Chapter 51

If possible, make a U-turn

"**R**ight," said Amy, after Jack went quiet. "Let's give it a go."

"One hundred and ninety-seven miles to destination."

"I think we better had," said Rahul.

Amy turned on the sat nav.

"If possible, make a U-turn," it said. For some reason, it now spoke in a woman's voice. Quite strict, a bit like a head teacher.

Nothing happened. The car carried on going.

"If possible, make a U-turn. You are driving away from your destination."

"One hundred and ninety-six miles to destination," said the drone from above.

"Oh, that's all right then!" said Janet.

"What?" said Jack.

"Well, the sat nav says we're driving away from our destination. But the drone says we're getting closer. And the drone's much shinier, and more hi-tech! So I believe it!"

"It's a different destination, Janet!" shouted Amy.

"Oh," said Janet. "Why is it called the same thing, then?"

"It's not working, Rahul!" said Amy, desperately trying to turn the steering wheel.

"Do you mean Janet's brain?" said Jack.

Janet stared at him, and put two fingers at her

eyes and then moved the fingers towards him.

Rahul shook his head. "It's not loud enough. I don't think the drone can hear it up there."

"You know it's not actually a person, right?" said Jack.

"Can we make it louder?" said Amy, ignoring her brother.

"Er . . ." Rahul looked around. "Yeah!" he said.

He got out a screwdriver and started fiddling with the dashboard.

"One hundred and ninety-five miles to destination."

"Do we . . . um . . . have time for like . . . doing mechanical work on the car?" said Amy.

"Just give me a moment . . ." said Rahul.

"Shall we sing something while we're waiting?" said Janet.

"Oh my days," said Jack.

"I don't know that one," said Janet. "What about 'Whistle While You Work'?"

She started whistling the tune to "Whistle While You Work".

"One hundred and ninety-four miles to destination," went the drone.

"Whistle whistle whistle. Whistle whistle whistle," went Janet.

"Wow. You're very good at whistling, Janet," said Amy.

"If possible, make a U-turn," said the sat nav.

"I think I may go mad," said Jack.

"OK!" said Rahul, pulling the sat nav free from the dashboard. There were wires behind it, but they were quite long, and he was able to hold it up in the air. "Done it!"

Rahul held the sat nav up further towards the roof of the TurboChaser. Then he pressed it against the bottom of the air horn. "With a bit of luck, that should amplify the sound enough."

"One hundred and ninety-three miles to destination."

Then very loudly, coming out through the horn,

like a loudspeaker placed above the car, the sat nav said, **"REPLACE THE UNIT IN THE DASHBOARD. YOU ARE A THIEF. SOMEONE IS BREAKING INTO THIS CAR. HELP! HELP!"**

"Oh dear," said Rahul.

Chapter 52

One hundred and ninety-two and a half miles

"**P**OLICE! POLICE! SAT NAV BEING STOLEN!"
said the sat nav very loudly.

"Maybe you should take it away from the air
horn?" said Jack.

"One hundred and ninety-two miles to destination."

"*Whistle whistle whistle . . .*"

"Why are you still whistling?" said Jack. "Rahul's idea's
not even *working* any more! In fact, *nothing* is working!
It's over! This adventure is over, and we've lost!"

"Don't say that!" said Amy.

"WEEOOOWEEOOOWEEOOO!" said the sat nav.

"Oh great," said Amy. "Now the sat nav's making a burglar alarm noise."

"At least it's covering up Janet's whistling," said Jack.

"Should I put it down?" said Rahul. "Turn it off?"

"Hold on," said Amy. "Hold your nerve."

"One hundred and ninety-one miles to destination."

"Come on, sat nav," said Amy.

"WEEOOOWEEOOOWEEOOO!"

"Come on. Just stop doing that for a second and remember what your *job* is. Come on!"

"WEEEOOOWWEEOOOWEEOO – if possible, make a U-turn," said the sat nav.

The drone stopped. Which meant the TurboChaser stopped. Everyone inside held their breath.

"If possible, make a U-turn."

The lights on the drone flickered. Almost like two eyes blinking. It was as if it was thinking about it. It hovered there for some time.

"Come on," said Amy.

"Come on," said Jack.

"Come on," said Rahul.

"Whistle whistle whistle," said Janet.

And then, the drone flew up in the air. Up and around. It did what the sat nav told it to do. It made a U-turn. A big, flowing U-turn – and then it started flying in the opposite direction.

The Taylor TurboChaser followed suit.

"YES!" shouted the children.

"One hundred and ninety-two miles to destination," said the drone.

"I can't believe that worked!" said Jack.

"It was a long shot!" said Rahul. "But it did the trick!"

Jack leant over and high-fived Rahul.

"One hundred and ninety-two and a half miles to destination," said the drone.

"Is it going to be following us all the way to my

dad's now?" said Amy.

"One hundred and ninety-three miles to desti— One hundred and ninety-four miles to desti— Mobilcon going away from destination— Job requirement to go other way— But new instruction to U-turn override— Malfunction! Malfunction! Malfunction!"

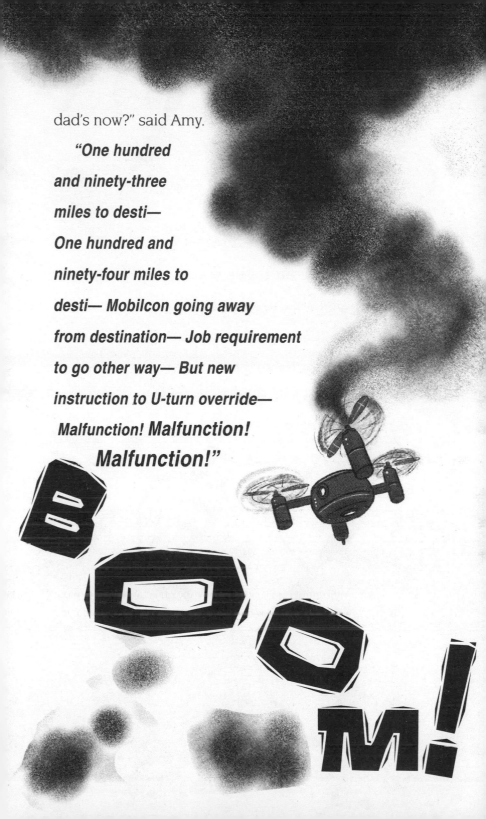

The drone exploded. Tiny bits of it – lights, fans, metal – rained down on the TurboChaser's roof.

"Don't think so," said Jack.

"Please rejoin the route to your destination," said the sat nav.

"Which one is that?" said Janet.

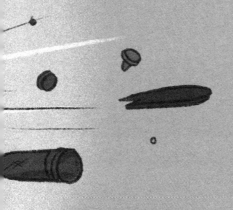

Chapter 53

And I'll take the low road

It was the last leg of the journey. The roads became long and straight and carved their way between some very high hills.

Soon they found themselves approaching signs that said,

Then

Then

I mean, I don't think I can make it any plainer –
they were getting closer to Scotland.

"We're nearly there!" said Janet.

"Well, not quite," said Amy. "My dad's place isn't
right on the border."

"Are we going to where he lives?" said Rahul.

"No," said Amy. "We're going to where he works."

"Why?"

"You'll see when we get there," said Amy.

"So how far from the border is that?" said Janet.

"Not far. Well, actually I'm not sure. But I know a man who does. Or at least the voice of a man. Or a woman."

She pressed the sat nav button.

"You take the High Road . . ." it sang.

"Oh!" said Amy.

"And I'll take the Low Road . . ."

"Why is it Scottish now?"

"I think it might have a program where it does whatever accent suits where it is," said Rahul.

"And I'll be in Scotland afore ye," it continued.

"Well, you won't, Mrs Sat Nav," said Jack. "Unless something very strange happens, we will both be in Scotland at the same time."

"This isn't telling us how much further we have to go," said Janet.

"Yes. I've just realised that's because it's the radio," said Amy. She pressed another button.

"Stay on this road for twelve miles," said the sat nav in a completely normal sat nav voice. "Then you will have reached your final destination."

"HOORAY!" shouted all the children at once.

And this was when the Taylor TurboChaser made its most painful-sounding noise yet – not a groan but more of a long, extended whimper – and then ground to a complete halt.

"Oh dear," said Amy.

Chapter 54

Not very nice

The TurboChaser trundled off to the side of the road. Amy – and Janet and Jack – looked to Rahul.

"ETA at destination 13:47 based on current road speed," said the sat nav.

"*Aaargh!*" said Amy. "Dad's leaving at midday."

"Hmm," said Rahul. "Try turning it on and off again."

"Really?" said Jack.

"Really," said Rahul.

"Yes, the problem with that, Rahul . . ." said Amy, ". . . is that it *is* off. And what I'm doing now, and have, in fact, been doing for about a minute, is pressing the 'on' switch." She did so again. "And as you can see, nothing is happening."

"Oh dear," said Rahul.

"That's what Amy said," said Janet.

"OK," said Jack. "So what do you think is wrong?"

"Well," said Rahul, "I could get out and look under the bonnet and spend a lot of time tinkering about, but I think I know what it is. We've run out of gas."

"Gas?" said Janet. "I thought it runs on a battery."

"It does." He pulled open the little door in the dashboard, the one with the red switch inside. It felt quite a long time ago now since Amy had first flipped that switch. "A turbocharged battery, if you remember. And this door is marked

ONLY IN EMERGENCIES." He looked round. "We've had it on the whole time."

Jack and Amy exchanged glances. "Well," said Amy, "it kind of *was* an emergency most of the time."

"So it's a gas battery?" said Janet.

"No! It's an electric battery!" said Rahul. "And it's run out of electricity! I was using 'gas' as a sort of metaphorical catch-all term for power!"

"What?" said Janet.

"Never mind!"

"So what are we going to do?" said Amy, looking around. "I can see a lot of hills, and grass, and cars passing us by, but no charging points."

"OK . . . well, I did think this might happen," said Rahul. "So I do have an idea."

"Oh no. Please, no," said Janet.

"You don't have to say that every time I say, 'I have an idea'," said Rahul, getting out of the car. He went round the back and opened the old chest. Then he came back to the front again, dragging a large plastic crate. With something inside it. Something . . . not very nice-looking.

"Ahh, I didn't know this would be so heavy."

Amy wrinkled her nose. "What IS that?"

"Poo," said Rahul.

"Yes," said Amy. "It does smell. But what is it?"

"No, it *is* poo. Cow poo. Do you remember? I scraped loads of it off the back of the TurboChaser when we went through that field of cattle."

"What?" said Jack. "And it's been in the car the whole time? And *I'm* the one who gets blamed for the smell! When that's been giving off poo gas the whole time? Well, thanks very much!"

"So why did Rahul say we'd run out of gas?" said Janet.

"OH HEAVENS!" said Rahul. "IT'S JUST AN EXPRESSION! SOMETHING PEOPLE SAY! But . . ." he continued, calming down, "as it happens, we kind of *will* be running on gas now. If my idea works out. Because one thing cow poo contains is of course . . . methane! Which is a gas. Through which we can make the poo into a biofuel. Well done, Janet!"

"Thanks!" said Janet. "I have no idea what you're talking about!"

"So . . ." said Rahul. "Who's going to help me get this poo out of the crate and into the right part of the engine?"

The other children looked at each other.

Then, very deliberately, Amy put her hand up.

And said, "I can't. I'm disabled."

Chapter 55

 **Believe**

In the end, Amy did help, holding the bonnet – it wasn't really a bonnet. It was lots of metal trays welded together, but it served as a bonnet – up.

Meanwhile, Rahul twiddled around underneath, and Janet and Jack were given the job of lifting up the cow-poo crate, ready to pour.

"Hold your end higher!" shouted Janet.

"What, closer to my nose?" said Jack.

"It has to be diagonal for us to pour it!"

"Oh, suddenly you're an expert at geometry?"

"I'll slam you up against *me tree* in a minute!"

"That is literally the worst joke I have ever heard!"

"I'm laughing at it," said Amy.

"Can you two stop arguing?" said Rahul. "And you stop laughing, Amy – I'm trying to concentrate!" He bent down, and then gestured for them to step forward. He had put a funnel into a section of the engine. "OK . . . into there. Pour the manure!"

And they did. While both going, "UUURR-GGGHHHH!"

A few seconds later, they were all back in the car.

"OK, Amy," said Rahul, "let's try and start her up again."

"Do you think it's going to work?"

Rahul shook his head. "Only one way to find out."

Amy nodded, and pressed the "on" switch.

Nothing happened.

"Oh dear," said Rahul.

"No," said Amy. "Come on. It's like the sat nav. We have to believe this will work."

"Yes, everybody," said Jack. "Believe in poo."

Amy turned round. "SHUT UP, JACK!"

Jack started doing his stupid voice: "SHUT U—"

"I MEAN IT. SHUT UP. I HAVE HAD ENOUGH OF YOU BEING SARCASTIC AND CYNICAL AND THINKING IT'S FUNNY JUST TO REPEAT STUFF BACK IN A STUPID VOICE. OK, SOMETIMES IT IS FUNNY. BUT NOT ALWAYS. IF YOU'RE MY BROTHER, AND YOU LOVE ME, YOU WILL DO WHAT I SAY, WHICH IS, TO BELIEVE THAT THIS WILL WORK."

There was a pause, during which Jack looked a little ashamed.

"You sound like Mum," he said sulkily. "With her silly quotes about how if you believe in your dreams, they'll all come true."

"Yes," said Amy. "They *are* silly. But you know what? A lot of her quotes have come into my head all through this journey. And they've helped. They really have. So . . . please, Jack."

He looked at her. "OK," he said. "I'll give it a go."

"I was believing it already," said Janet.

"Thank you, Janet," said Amy.

"Although that didn't work."

"Yes, it might if we do it all together, though. Ready. Steady . . ." She turned back to the steering wheel. "BELIEVE!"

And they all did. Jack even closed his eyes. Janet scrunched her face up, as if she was believing really hard.

And Amy flicked the "on" switch.
And
    nothing
        happened.

Chapter 56

The ready, steady

"**O**h," Amy said. "That always works in films and stuff."

There was a pause. No one quite knew what to say.

Then Rahul said, "You could try it again."

"OK," said Amy. She flicked the switch, off and then on. And it worked! The engine fired and the car, with another big groan, trembled into life!

"Brilliant!" said Rahul.

"Amazing!" said Amy.

"Fantastic!" said Jack.

"I wasn't believing then, though," said Janet.

"Oh, I was," said Jack.

"So was I," said Rahul.

"Well, I wasn't!" said Janet. "I wasn't ready. You didn't do the build-up. Y'know – the ready, steady . . . you didn't do that."

"OK," said Amy.

"But I don't really feel I did anything now."

"Sorry."

"Can you turn it off and do it again?" said Janet.

Amy shook her head and drove back on to the road, towards Scotland.

"ETA 11:45 at destination," said the sat nav.

"Yay!" said Amy.

Chapter 57

Sort of like a friend

The Taylor Automotive Test Facility, an offshoot of Taylor Automotive Design, was a large black building at the top of a hill. Behind it was a long, wide track that twisted and turned into many shapes.

Because the Taylor Automotive Test Facility was a place Peter Taylor took the cars he had designed – very fast supercars, if you remember – to test them out. Raced them, basically. Yes. People actually get paid to do that.

Amy was very excited when it came into view. They drove round the corner of the road from the border – the children all cheered when they went past the **WELCOME TO SCOTLAND** sign – and saw the Facility, some way above them. It helped to take their minds off the smell of burning cow poo, which was suffusing the inside of the car.

"That's it, isn't it?" Amy said to Jack. "Where Dad works."

"I think so. I was only eight."

"Haven't *you* ever been here before, Amy?" said Rahul.

Amy paused before saying, "No."

There was another pause, as she turned the Taylor TurboChaser off the main road, on to the smaller one leading up the hill. The sky was darkening slightly, as if it was about to rain.

"Dad came to live – and work – up here after he

and Mum split up," said Jack. "He brought me up once and showed me round, but . . . not Amy."

"He's sent me some photos, though," said Amy, sounding cheerful, in a slightly forced way. "And I've seen it on the internet."

No one said anything again. Except Janet, who said, "I feel sick."

The TurboChaser carried on up the hill. The road was very winding, and, as well as the bad smell emanating from the engine, the car was starting to make a lot of very strange noises – not just groans now, but squeals and grunts and scrapings. Plus it was shaking a lot, like it had a bad fever.

"Is it OK?" said Amy to Rahul.

Rahul shrugged.

"Because I really wouldn't want it to conk out now. Apart from anything," she continued, "I've come to think of it – the car – as part of our gang."

"How do you mean?"

"Well, sort of like a friend. Sort of like a real person. Is that stupid?"

"No," said Rahul. "I mean it's wrong. But it's not stupid."

The car shook again as he said this, but by now they were approaching the last corner, and then there they were outside the front of the building. Amy stopped the car, but she didn't turn off the engine just yet.

"You have reached your final destination," said the sat nav.

And the children all cheered. And they carried on cheering, right up until, from behind the building, came Suzi Taylor's van.

Chapter 58

Like a proper big brother

The van drove up to the TurboChaser.

"Quick!" said Janet. "Turn round."

Amy looked round behind her. As she suspected, the road back down the hill was now cut off by DCI Bryant's and PC Middleton's police car, and one other police car. They had clearly all been waiting for them, hiding behind the building.

"Oh no!" said Rahul.

"It's OK," said Amy. "There's no point in going

backwards, anyway. This is where we were heading. We're here now."

Out of the van came Suzi, Prisha, Sanjay, Colin and Norma. They walked over to the TurboChaser. With – in Suzi's case, because of Colin's enormous trousers – some difficulty.

"Amy . . . darling . . ." said Suzi through the side cat flap, having finally got to the car. "I know this has been something you really wanted to do – something really important to you – and I know you were desperate to show your dad how good at driving you are – but—"

"Oh, for goodness' sake, Suzi!" said Prisha. "Stop talking to them like they're teddy bears! RAHUL! GET OUT OF THAT STUPID CONTRAPTION NOW! HOW DARE YOU PUT US THROUGH ALL THIS, YOU BAD BOY! COME ON! GET OUT!"

Rahul turned to Amy. "I think . . . I'd better get out."

Amy nodded. She touched his arm. "Thanks, Rahul . . . for everything. For this amazing journey."

Rahul smiled. "Thank you, Amy." He shimmied through his cat flap and out of the car.

"Hey! Janet!" said Norma. "How's things?"

"Fine, Mum!"

"I've bought you some crisps!" said Colin, bringing out an enormous bag. "At a service station on the way. Baked-bean flavour!"

"Brilliant!" said Janet, and within seconds she was out too.

"Jack . . ." said Suzi, "I don't know what to say to you. I know I should tell you off for helping Amy do this . . . but at the same time I want to thank you for looking after her . . . and, anyway, if I start talking seriously to you, you'll just be sarcastic—"

"I won't, actually, Mum," said Jack. He made to get out of the car. Just before he did, he put his arm on Amy's shoulder. She looked round. He winked at her. "You did well," he said, like a proper big brother.

Then, finally, he got out.

Amy watched as Rahul went over to his mum and dad. It looked for a second like Prisha, who raised her hand, was going to slap him round the head, but then she gave him a big hug instead. Suzi also gave Jack a big hug, although he looked a bit embarrassed about that.

And Janet just tucked into her crisps, helped by Norma and Colin, almost as if she'd never been away.

Then they all turned to look at Amy.

"Shall we come and help you get out, Amy?" said Suzi.

Amy shook her head.

"Amy . . ." said Suzi.

Amy shook her head again. A black cloud appeared above the Facility.

"Amy, please . . ."

"No, Mum. I'm not getting out," she said. "Sorry, Mum. I'm not getting out until—"

"Amy," said her parent again.

Only it was a much deeper voice. And a different parent.

From out of the front doors of the building stepped – tall, wearing a black boiler suit, and frowning angrily – Peter Taylor.

Chapter 59

A strange decision

Amy watched her dad come towards the TurboChaser. She noticed he was also holding a crash helmet. She was frightened, but decided to pretend she wasn't.

"Hi, Dad!" she said, waving from inside the car. "Cool helmet! Can I have a look?"

He tutted, but handed it through the cat flap.

"Amy," said her dad, as she ran her hands over the top of the helmet. "This is ridiculous. This whole thing. Doing all –" he waved a hand towards the body of the TurboChaser – "*this* to your wheelchair. And then driving it all the way up here! I can't believe you made it! Even though I instructed Mobilcon to send out a retrieval drone!"

"Oh, that was . . . you . . ."

"I have no idea what happened to it."

"Um. Yeah. Me neither," said Amy.

"But that aside, it was *far* too dangerous for you to do this journey! With all these other children, including your brother! And – oh my God, *what* is that terrible smell? Anyway . . . what on *earth* were you thinking of?"

Amy looked at his cross, scrunched face, his wagging, raised finger. And it came to her what the answer to his question was.

I was thinking of YOU, Dad. I was thinking that I wanted you to see my amazing wheelchair-car. I wanted you to see how good I am at driving it. I suppose I thought

that if you saw all that, you might think that I was . . . I
don't know . . . what you want me to be.

That's what I was thinking of.

But she didn't say any of that. Instead, she just drove off, leaving him standing there, open-mouthed.

She didn't know where she was going. She also couldn't *see* where she was going, as her eyes had filled with tears.

But she knew the one thing she felt OK about at the moment was driving. She felt like, despite the admittedly terrible smell, everything might be fine, as long as she could drive and never stop. Or at least, never get out of the car.

Wiping her eyes, she could see, behind her, Suzi and the other parents get back into the van. Worryingly, she could also see the police cars moving off. A*nd* her dad, putting on a new helmet, joined by two other men in boiler suits. She drove as fast as she could round the Facility building. On the other side of it she could see, beneath her, the racing track. There was a small paved road that led directly to it.

The black cloud that had been hanging in the sky for a while burst, and it began to rain hard.

Amy drove down the hill to the racing track. Then she made what some might think is a strange decision. She turned on to the track, which was fenced on either side, there was a black and white line painted across it – a starting line.

She stopped the TurboChaser there, put on the crash helmet, and waited.

Chapter 60

Sitting wide

She only had to wait about thirty seconds before her mum's van, two police cars and three supercars came charging down the road towards the track. Amy recognised the supercars straight away – they were Taylor GT 500s, her dad's fastest design yet – all three were sparkling silver-grey and sat so low to the road (to reduce wind speed) they were almost flat.

Just as the chasing convoy reached the starting

line, Amy pushed the direction lever, revving the engine.

"You have reached your final destination," said the sat nav again.

"Apparently not," said Amy. And shot away.

Immediately, the van, the police cars and the supercars gave chase. Amy pumped the lever as hard as she could. The TurboChaser screamed, but it moved.

Wow, did it move.

She had not been able, on the small country roads that they had driven on so far, to really push the engine and see how fast it could go. But now, on this wide racing track, she could.

Oh my days. What is the actual acceleration on this, Amy found herself thinking, despite the situation, *0–60 in three seconds?*

But there was no time to indulge her inner petrolhead. She had to concentrate. The rain seemed to have stopped almost as soon as it had started, but it had left the road wet and greasy. The TurboChaser was shuddering with the speed.

Meanwhile, in front of her, was the first turn on the track. It didn't just turn hard, it banked – it rose

to one side, on a steep diagonal. This meant she had to throw her weight to the side. Otherwise she could feel, on the wet road, the whole machine would've gone into a skid! How did she know to do this? It just seemed to come to her naturally.

Other people, however, did not know it.

As Amy banked round the turn and shot off into the long straight that followed it, she just saw, out of the corner of her rear-view mirror, DCI Bryant's car go into that very skid.

"AAAAAARGGGGGHHHH!" shouted DCI Bryant, as they went spinning round and round and round.

"Turn the steering wheel the other way, sir!" shouted PC Middleton.

"Are you sure? Aren't you supposed to turn the steering wheel INTO a skid? AAARRGGH! WHAT DOES THAT EVEN MEAN?"

"DO SOMETHING, SIR!"

"I'M TRY—"

BANG! The -ING of "TRYING" was lost as their car smashed into the side of a supercar driven by one of Peter Taylor's test drivers. Both cars now went into a spin and ended up on the side of the track, taking the other police car with them.

But Amy didn't even see all that.

She was speeding down the end of the straight and starting to bank in the other direction. She could see, in her rear-view mirror, the two remaining supercars hard on her heels. Even with all that going on in her head, she thought, *They look amazing! So sleek and streamlined, like two leopards chasing a hyena.*

Then it occurred to her that, in this analogy, she was the hyena – the prey. Which made her push on the lever even harder. She felt the wheels shudder underneath her, and again the car shook round the bank, but – again – she shifted her weight and got it under control.

The last bend before coming back to the starting line was what on racing tracks is called a hairpin – meaning it's shaped a bit like a hairpin, with a very sharp bend – and turning it at speed without crashing is very difficult. But Amy couldn't slow down because the supercars were gaining on her.

So she didn't even brake – she just powered into the turn, going round as wide as possible, almost hitting the fence . . . but then pulling the car round at the last second and back into the home straight.

And then she saw, coming up, another problem – her mum's van. Which Suzi had – sensibly, given that it was a van (top speed 53 mph, acceleration 0–53 . . . in about six minutes) – decided not to enter into this strange race, but rather had left idling, sitting tight, on the starting line, waiting for her daughter and the TurboChaser to come back round again.

When I say "sitting tight", what I actually mean is sitting *wide*. The van was parked *across* the starting line. Blocking the way. And Suzi, Sanjay, Prisha, Colin and Norma had got out and were standing on either side of it, holding hands. And their faces were set.

Amy looked to the side to see if she could swerve past them by going back on to the paved road from the Facility.

But the opening in the fence that led to the track had been shut. There was no way to go but forward.

Amy looked at her mum. She swallowed.

"This is your final destination," said the sat nav again.

"*Please* stop saying that," said Amy.

Chapter 61

Baked-bean-flavour crisps

The TurboChaser was heading directly either straight for the van or for one of the parents. It was a stand-off, a game of chicken. And, so far, none of the parents looked like they were going to chicken out. In a terrible moment, which she felt immediately bad about, it did cross Amy's mind to think, *Would anyone really miss Colin and Norma?* And then she realised, yes, someone would – Janet.

Amy carried on heading directly towards them,

hoping that at least one of the parents would break. Sanjay in particular didn't look too happy – his eyes were flashing towards Prisha in a very "Are you *sure* about this?" kind of way. Amy could see her mum as well, who though she appeared brave and steadfast, was also, from the look in her eyes, pleading. Pleading for Amy to just stop the car and give up.

But she wasn't ready to do that. Not yet. And, behind her, she could see the supercars getting very close now. Then she noticed something. Colin and Norma had stopped holding hands. Because Colin, it turned out, had another enormous packet of baked-bean-flavour crisps, and had chosen this moment to stuff a few into his mouth.

Both Amy's hands were gripped tight on the steering wheel. In a flash, she lifted her right hand off, and reached over to press the button she needed.

From the parents' point of view, the vehicle that was coming straight for them suddenly got much thinner and more like a rocket. All the wheels went into a single line, and the motorbike version of the TurboChaser swerved at the last minute away

from the van and, with a *whoosh!*, snaked through
the small gap between Colin and Norma created by
Colin's need to eat crisps.

"What happened there?" said Colin, looking up, munching.

Chapter 62

Until she absolutely has to

On the other side of the starting line, the two supercars, unable to get past, had stopped. Suzi walked over to speak to Peter. He took off his helmet.

"Hmm," said Peter. "This isn't as easy as I thought it would be."

"No," said Suzi. "Things often aren't as easy as *you* think they'll be."

Peter stared at her.

"What's that supposed to mean?"

She stared back at him. "Well, Peter. I think you probably thought after the accident that the *easiest* way of dealing with your guilt about it was to leave your family and go and live miles away."

"I—" he began.

"I think you thought it was *easier* because that way you wouldn't have to be confronted every day with your disabled daughter."

Peter went very red, and opened his mouth to speak. He looked extremely angry.

"Or with me," said a voice, "and the fact that I was also pretty shaken up by the accident."

They turned. It was Jack who had spoken. He looked nervous. But suddenly older, not so much like a stretched-out toddler – as if he'd suddenly become a little bit more of a man.

Peter Taylor shook his head. Jack's interruption

had cut off his anger. Perhaps because it was the first time Jack had said anything to him for some time. Now he looked more confused. "I can't believe that's what you think!" he said.

"It is what we think, Dad. It's what we *all* think. Well, except Amy. Who probably does think it too, but wouldn't say it."

"Yes, Peter," said Suzi. "Because she loves you too much."

He opened his mouth again. But then he shut it and, for a second, just looked very, very sad.

Suzi sighed and put a hand on his shoulder. "Having said that, blaming each other is not helping. As it never does. It's not getting our daughter out of that vehicle and into a safe place."

Peter nodded. He turned back to the track. "Well," he said, "I suppose we could just sit here and wait for her to come round again."

Suzi looked out at the TurboChaser going round

the first bend of the track once more. It had gone back to its usual shape.

"No," she said. "Look."

He looked. The TurboChaser was slowing down. It stopped, about halfway round the track.

"I thought she might do that," said Suzi. "She'll just sit there now, until we chase her again."

"Why?"

Suzi took a deep breath. "Because I know my daughter. And she's trying to show you something. She's trying to show you she can *drive*. She's not going to stop until she absolutely has to."

Peter shook his head. "So – if you know her so much better than I do, Suzi – what do you suggest?"

Suzi blinked. She looked round. "Isn't it obvious?"

"Not to me."

"I'm going to take the van and the other parents off the track. I suggest you tell your other driver to get off too."

Peter frowned. "Leaving just me and her?"

"Yes. That's what she wants. To race you."

Peter thought about it. He almost, for a second, seemed to smile. Then he said, "OK."

Chapter 63

A chance

Amy watched from the other side of the track. She saw her dad open the fence by the starting line. She saw the van and the other supercar drive off the track.

Then her dad closed the fence and went back to his car. Before he put his helmet on, he shouted, "Amy! Drive round here to the starting line. One lap. Just me and you! OK?"

Amy frowned. She didn't know what to do. Was

it a trap? Then again, she knew that, soon, the TurboChaser was going to run out of cow-poo-based biofuel, so what did she have to lose? And she could see her dad putting his helmet on and getting into his car. So, not quite sure why she was doing it, she did a thumbs-up at him, and moved the TurboChaser slowly round the track.

As she got near the starting line, she could hear the sound of the exhaust from her dad's car as he revved up. The sound was loud and powerful. Amy gulped.

I can't beat the GT 500 for pure speed, she thought. *And also, he's a brilliant driver.*

But before she even had a chance to worry about that, she was there, level with him.

He looked over at her. She saw his eyes, through the plastic visor of his helmet. They looked at her curiously – a new look she'd never seen from her dad before, but she couldn't say exactly what it was, and didn't have time to think about it.

What she *was* thinking about, very, very quickly, was a chance. She had no idea if it was going to work, but she went for it. As she passed him at the starting line, before he had a chance to set off, she pressed the tent button and the motorbike button *together*. The folds of coloured material started pouring out of the chimney, but the TurboChaser narrowed sharply at the same time – cutting off the tent material!

The tent flew like a spinning top all the way out of the chimney. It hovered for a second above Peter Taylor's car – he looked up from the driver's seat, confused – then flopped down on it, covering it like a big blanket.

"Bye, Dad!" shouted Amy, and drove towards the first bend. "See you at the finish line!"

Chapter 64

Ole′!

It only gained her a few seconds. Her dad pressed hard on his accelerator, and his GT 500 roared out from underneath its multicoloured blanket, so fast that the cloth flew back in the air as if a giant was throwing it over his shoulder.

Amy was already turning on the first bank, but she was well used to that turn by now, and cut in hard to the corner, maximising her speed but also minimising (sorry about the big words – making it big, making it little) the distance she had to go round as she did so.

Amy still knew it was no good trying to beat her father's supercar on speed alone. It was going to be all about skill. She was aware of him right behind her as she came out of the corner and into the straight. She swerved, blocking his way. He tried to take her on the right, but she moved right; then he threw his car round sharply to the left, but she had anticipated that, and jammed the back of the TurboChaser in front of the nose of his car again.

"Wow!" said Norma, watching (all the parents and the police and the other children had gone to sit in a little spectator stand behind the fence near the starting line). "Your daughter is a *really* good driver!"

Despite herself – and despite all the trouble Amy's driving ability had caused – Suzi found herself smiling inside at that.

"*Olé!*" shouted Colin, as the TurboChaser continued to block the GT 500's attempts at overtaking. Every time the supercar shifted even a millimetre to get past, the TurboChaser seemed to know which way it was going, and get there first.

"Why are you shouting '*Olé!*'?" said Janet. "Are you about to sing that Spanish song we all like?"

"No," said Colin. "When I go and see my football team play, sometimes when they pass the ball really well, and the other team can't get a touch, that's what the crowd shouts. '*Olé!*' they shout, every time one of our team gets the ball. So I'm doing it now, every time she blocks his way." He looked up. "*Olé!*"

Amy blocked her dad again, going into the second bend.

"*Olé!*" shouted Colin, and so did Jack, not as a sarcastic repeat, but because he was joining in.

Amy blocked Peter again!

"*Olé!*" shouted Sanjay and Janet, and Rahul did as well.

And again she blocked him, coming out into the straight!

Prisha, frowning, as if not sure she should, went, "*Olé!*" She paused. "Sorry. Do you mind that I'm supporting Amy?" she added, turning to Suzi. "I mean, obviously, this is dangerous and everything, and I don't condone that, but—"

"I don't mind at all," said Suzi, before shouting, along with all of them – as Amy swung the TurboChaser round *again* to hold up the GT 500 – "*OLÉ!*"

Chapter 65

WHAT'S HAPPENING?

Despite the cheers of her supporters, things were not easy for Amy. It was getting hot in the TurboChaser, and hot, with this particular fuel, also meant very, very smelly. But she was still in front of Peter and the GT 500, as the hairpin bend, the last corner before the finishing line, came into view.

"I can't do this any more," she said out loud to herself. "I can't block him on that bend. The corner's too tight!" Amy felt suddenly dizzy. She didn't know why –

she'd never before suffered from motion sickness. But maybe the G-force (that's a force that presses on you in cars and rockets when you go really fast) and the fumes and speed together were getting too much for her.

Perhaps she should just . . . stop, she thought. She was tired – exhausted – and she'd come a very long way. Maybe this was far enough. Maybe she'd done all she could. Maybe it was time to lie down and go to sleep. But then . . .

"You can do it!" said a voice, a female voice.

Amy frowned. "Who said that?"

"You can reach the finishing line! I know you can, Amy!"

She looked down.

"The sat nav?" she said.

"Yes!"

"You're speaking to me?"

"I'm the voice of the car! I'm the Taylor TurboChaser!"

"What?" said Amy.

"You can do it, Amy! You're a brilliant driver!"

OK, Amy thought. *It is the G-force and the fumes and the speed. I'm going mad.* But still, she replied, "I'm not. I'm just . . . just a girl in a wheelchair."

"No!" said the sat nav. "You're not. You're a brilliant driver!"

Amy shook her head. Which made her feel even dizzier. As it shook, she saw, out of the corner of her eye, her mum, standing by the side of the track now, with her hands clenched in front of her.

"You just have to believe it, Amy!" said the sat nav. "Only those who dare to fail greatly, achieve greatly! Trust your instincts, they'll never betray you!" And then it said, louder even than before, "I get knocked down, but I get up again!"

Amy's head stopped shaking. Something very weird was going on. The voice from the sat nav . . . it was *her* voice, and her mum's voice, and *her* thoughts, and her mum's thoughts, all mixed up . . . But also, on some level, she felt it was indeed the voice of the car, of the Taylor TurboChaser.

And it helped. It really, really helped. It focused her mind and made her believe in herself. It gave her an idea. As she went into the bend, she could see that her dad was edging round to her right. The front bonnet of the GT 500 was just getting ahead, by a few centimetres.

Oh no.

There were millimetres in it. But he was going to win.

"You get knocked down . . ." said the sat nav. "But you, Amy Taylor, *you* – you get back up again!"

And that was it. Amy gritted her teeth.

She pressed the motorbike button. The TurboChaser narrowed and extended; and, just by doing that, *she* was ahead again! Which meant that her dad couldn't pass her, as he hoped, at the point in the bend! Amy kept the motorbike shape going through the bend, just ahead, and then, as she came through into the home straight, pushed the button again to return the car to its normal shape. She pushed on the lever, heading for home.

Only the TurboChaser *didn't* head for home. It flipped suddenly back to motorbike shape. Then normal shape. Then motorbike shape. Every second, it narrowed, then widened.

"WHAT'S HAPPENING?" said Amy.

"URRRGHHH! I DON'T KNOW!" said the sat nav. "I DON'T FEEL VERY WELL!"

"Neither do I," said Amy because, suddenly, the car was starting to spin. As it did so, the two red hazard flags popped out, waving madly. The TurboChaser *kept* flipping shape, between thin and wide, so fast now that it was jolting Amy each time.

"Um . . ." said Jack, "is it meant to be doing that?"

"Oh yeah," said Colin. "Clearly it's another bit of amazing skill!"

It wasn't. But it *was* keeping Peter Taylor from overtaking. The spinning, the flagging, the changing shape – it was all making it impossible for him to judge how to get round the car. And Amy was only ten metres from the line. Through her own nausea, she gripped the steering wheel.

"COME ON, TURBOCHASER! YOU CAN DO IT! JUST HOLD IT TOGETHER!"

"URRRRGH! I'M TRYING!"

"COME ON, AMY!" shouted Suzi.

"YES! OLÉ! AMY! AMY! AMY! AMY!" shouted the others.

The TurboChaser spun and spun and spun and spun and spun . . . and then the sat nav said quietly, in a voice that sounded all cracked and tinny and like it was gasping for breath, "I'm so sorry, Amy . . . I really am."

At which point, a metre from the finishing line, the Taylor TurboChaser fell completely to pieces.

"OH NO! AMY!" screamed Suzi, rushing from the stand.

Chapter 66

Always fine

From Suzi's point of view, it had suddenly become clear that the spin/flag/shape-shifting thing was not a clever driving tactic after all, but a sign of the TurboChaser malfunctioning in a very bad way, before finally giving up the ghost.

Most of it had fallen away, leaving only Amy spinning by the finishing line, in just her original new electronic wheelchair.

The Mobilcon XR-207. With no add-ons at all.

That was all that was left of it. Around her lay many fish tanks and trays and mattresses and chimneys and power torches. Meanwhile, Peter Taylor's GT 500 stopped next to her.

"She pushed it too far!" shouted Rahul, running after Suzi.

"We all pushed it too far!" shouted Jack, running after Rahul.

"I've run out of crisps!" shouted Colin.

The parents and the children all ran over towards Amy, still in her chair, motionless, with her helmet on.

Then a loud, metallic voice said, "EXCUSE ME, EVERYONE! STEP AWAY FROM THE INJURED PARTY!"

"Oh, you got the megaphone working again, sir!" said PC Middleton.

"Yes, Middleton," said DCI Bryant, holding it up. "Just needed some new batteries and a little bit of technical know-how, and—"

"ZIP IT, DCI BRYANT!" shouted Prisha. "WE NEED TO CONCENTRATE ON AMY!"

"Oh."

Peter was the first to get to her. "Amy? Are you . . ."

But Amy waved him away. She waved all of them away. "Give me a minute," she said.

They stood there, staring at her.

"*Give me a minute,*" she said.

She looked at the finish line, just a metre in front of her. Then down at the debris around her. Then she pressed the lever forward. Nothing happened.

I get knocked down. But I get up again.

Slowly, she put a hand on each wheel. It wasn't designed, this chair – not like her old chair – to be pushed like that. It was supposed to be electric.

She felt the heavy resistance of the wheels.

I get knocked down. But I get up again.

"Amy . . ." said her mum, concerned.

"Wait . . ." said Amy, breathing heavily.

Slowly – very slowly – the chair began to move forward, crunching over glass and plastic.

Rahul ran over to push – but Amy shook her head.

She rolled herself painstakingly, painfully, past the watching crowd of parents and police and friends – past the broken scattered pieces of the TurboChaser –

– and over the line.

Everyone cheered.

Even Peter.

And Amy lowered her hands, exhausted, her chin flopping on her chest. With an effort, she lifted her helmet off her head. She was very conscious that she was sitting there in just a wheelchair, bits of metal and glass and wiring behind her.

Her dad rushed up. "Amy! Are you OK? That was—"

"Yes, Dad, I'm fine."

"Oh. Good. Nothing broken?"

Amy looked up at him. She was tired and breathless, but her voice rang out clear. "No. The thing is . . . I'm *fine*, Dad. Not just now, but generally. I think you think I might be a bit broken. But I'm really not. I'm kind of . . . *always* fine."

Peter looked back at her. His eyes filled with tears.

Finally, after a long moment, he nodded.

"Oh, thank God, Amy," said Suzi, barging Peter out of the way, and falling on to her daughter and kissing her and hugging her. "I'm so glad you're OK! Because, if you weren't," she added, "I'd have *killed* you."

Chapter 67

A dodgem car by the sea

Suzi was smiling, though, and Amy laughed. Then they were both laughing. Until Amy's dad put his hand on her arm.

"Amy . . ." said Peter. "We still need to talk about . . . this." He indicated the broken bits of TurboChaser.

"I'm sorry, Dad," said Amy, disentangling herself from her mum. "I'm sorry I put you through all this. I hope all your cars are OK. I'm sorry I—"

"You're amazing."

". . . took all the other children and . . . Pardon?"

Peter shook his head in wonder. His eyes had that new way of looking at her that Amy had noticed earlier, the one that she couldn't think of the word for.

"I mean, absolutely," he said. "You shouldn't have done ANY of this – shouldn't have done all this to your wheelchair, shouldn't have put your mum through all this worry, but . . . we'll talk about all that afterwards. Because –" he shook his head and smiled – "you're *totally amazing*! What an incredible driver you are. I've never seen anything like it. You're a natural."

Amy smiled and blushed. She wanted to say, "Well, you have seen *something* like it, a long time ago, on a dodgem car by the sea." But instead she just let the words *"you're a natural"* fire up the memory of that moment again, and said, "Thank you, Dad."

"And, as your dad," he said, "let me give you a hug." Which he did, lifting her up off the chair and into his arms. He gave her the tightest hug.

"But also," he said, once he'd put her back into the chair, "as a fellow driver, let me shake your hand." He held out his. Amy took it. They shook hands. He looked at her and smiled.

"*Respect*," said Amy's dad. Which was the word that described, Amy realised, what was contained in her father's new way of looking at her.

Chapter 68

"Was that sarcastic?"

On the way back home, everyone managed to get into Suzi's van, even though it was a bit of a squeeze. It was a long drive. Prisha suggested they stop at a restaurant they'd found on the way up called La Rurale Pastorale, but none of the children were very keen for some reason.

Amy sat in her old wheelchair in the back. Her dad had told her to leave her new wheelchair, which didn't seem to work at all any more, with him. As they were nearing the end of the journey, Rahul said, "Do you think your dad will fix your wheelchair? Or buy you a new one?"

"I don't know," said Amy. "What about your dad? Is he cross that all that stuff from his warehouse got broken?"

Rahul looked round. Sanjay was asleep on Prisha's shoulder.

"No, he's OK. He's always OK as long as Mum isn't shouting at him. And, anyway, we went round picking up some bits that weren't broken and put them in the back of the van. He reckons if I can build another one, loads of people might want one . . ." The word "broken" seemed to make him feel suddenly sad. He tailed off and blinked.

"I'm sorry it all broke . . ." he said, "the TurboChaser."

Amy smiled. "That's fine. It's amazing it lasted so long."

Rahul smiled back. "It did last a long time, didn't

it? And went a long way."

Amy nodded. "It was a brilliant adventure. Thank you, Rahul."

He smiled. She looked round. Sanjay, as we know, was asleep. Janet was with Colin and Norma, showing them how she had actually learnt to turn her phone off. Jack was leaning over to the front of the van, talking to Suzi. Amy lowered her voice.

"Rahul . . . a weird thing happened just before the TurboChaser broke up."

Rahul frowned. "What?"

Amy lowered her voice even more, almost to a whisper. "The sat nav started talking to me . . ."

"Pardon?" said Rahul.

"I know it sounds stupid. But I was talking to myself, about how I didn't think I could win the race. And it started telling me that . . . I could."

"Wow."

Amy looked at him. "You don't believe me."

"Well. No. I do. I mean the sat nav was kind of weird."

Amy shook her head. "Yes. But it was still telling us where to go, or where not to go. It wasn't giving us a pep talk, or helping because it knew I was frightened." She looked at Rahul. "It was like at the last moment . . . the TurboChaser was really talking to me. Like it was really my friend."

Rahul nodded. He touched her on the shoulder. "Maybe it was."

A little while later, they were back in their home city. Suzi dropped Janet and Colin and Norma off back at their house first. Everyone said goodbye, but then Colin said, as they got out, "Janet! Where are your fairy wings?"

"They got covered in poo."

"Oh," said Norma. "Not again."

"No, they're clean now," said Rahul. "Remember

you washed them in the stream!"

Amy saw them by her feet. She picked them up.

"Here they are! Sparkling clean!"

She threw them out of the window of the van. They fluttered up in the air, glittering in the street light, before coming down like a butterfly, to land almost perfectly behind Janet. Norma clamped her hands on them, holding them to her daughter's back.

"Ha!" said Amy. "You were right! They've come in useful!"

"How is that useful?" said Jack.

"As a symbol of our journey!" said Amy.

Next, Suzi dropped Rahul, Sanjay and Prisha back at their flat above Agarwal Supplies. Sanjay and Rahul quickly took all the TurboChaser bits out of the back of the van, and then everyone said goodbye – a quick goodbye, as it was late by then and Suzi wanted to get her children finally home.

"Help your dad get that stuff back into the garage," said Prisha, going inside, "and then bedtime!"

"OK, Mum," said Rahul.

"What have we got left?" said Sanjay.

Rahul looked around. "One fish tank. Half a fish tank. Two walkie-talkies. Two giant cat flaps. Some tent material . . ."

"The mattresses, they're fine," said Sanjay.

"Well, they're a bit wet."

"They'll dry out. Ah, look," Sanjay said, picking something up. "The sat nav! The screen isn't broken!"

"Yes, but it's a bit of a weird one, anyway."

"Well, it was always a weird batch."

"Yes. Amy said it got even weirder during the race."

Sanjay looked at the bits and pieces of the TurboChaser. He smiled. "OK, son. So . . . is this the invention that's going to make us rich?"

Rahul smiled. "I don't think so, Dad. But who

knows?" He yawned. "Thanks for being so good about it all. Let's get this stuff into the warehouse so I can go to bed."

"Goodnight, Amy," said Suzi.

Amy was finally home, tucked up in bed. Her mum was crouching beside her.

"Are you really, really angry with me, Mum?" said Amy.

Suzi took a deep breath. "I was. Yes. I thought I was really going to shout at you. But now . . . all that anger . . . it's all gone. I'm exhausted, and I'm just so happy that you're home and safe."

"I'm sorry, Mum. I'm sorry I put you through all that."

Suzi looked at her daughter lying in bed, her head on the pillow. She kissed her on her forehead.

"It's OK, Amy. I kind of know why you had to do it. Just . . . don't do it again. Please."

Amy smiled. "I won't. I promise. I'll never do anything like that again."

Suzi nodded, said, "Thank you, darling," and left the room.

Ten seconds later, through the wall, Jack's voice said, "Was that sarcastic?"

Amy, even though she was nearly asleep, burst out laughing.

Chapter 69

You can't say no

Two months later, Amy was at home in the living room with her mum and Jack, helping to decorate their Christmas tree. A song called "Driving Home for Christmas" by a frightening-looking old man called Chris Rea was playing on the radio as she wheeled herself round the tree, draping the branches with baubles and tinsel.

She could do this easily, even though she was

back in her old wheelchair, as it had been fixed. The wheels no longer resembled that of a broken Lodlil trolley. The whole thing had been given an overhaul and now she could guide herself round even quite a small space, like that between their Christmas tree and the wall, easily.

Every year, Amy loved decorating the tree. Jack was bored of doing it – decorating a Christmas tree is one of those things teenagers used to love doing when they were younger, but which they like to make clear to parents that now they find *very* boring.

So he was huffing and puffing and looking at his phone, when there was suddenly the sound of something being delivered through their letter box.

"Can you go and see what that is, Jack?" said Suzi.

Jack huffed and puffed and looked at his phone – which meant he didn't want to do *that* either – but he went out of the room anyway.

"Oh right," he shouted from the hallway, in his

bored voice. "It's Dad's regular Christmas card."

"Oh!" said Amy. "Bring it in!"

"*Oh*," said Jack in a sarcastic voice, "*bring it in!*" (I should make it clear that although Jack had learnt *some* life lessons on this journey, he hadn't changed that much. Not everyone changes *that* much during a story.)

"Well . . . yeah, do," said Suzi.

"It'll just be the same thing as ever," said Jack, coming into the living room. He opened the envelope. "Just 'Happy Christmas, Jack and Amy!' on a card with some fake snow and glitter on . . . Oh— "

"What?" said Suzi.

"Some tickets have fallen out of it . . ."

Amy wheeled herself

over to them and picked them up. "They're train tickets! To Scotland!"

"What does the card say, Jack?" asked Suzi.

"It says, *'Dear Suzi, Jack and Amy . . .'*"

"Can you read it in a normal voice, please? Not a stupid one."

"Hmm . . . OK. 'Dear Suzi, Jack and Amy, I was wondering if you might want to come to Scotland for Christmas? And spend it with me? You don't have to, but if you do, some rail tickets are enclosed . . . Love, Dad." He looked up and, for once, his eyes were like a child's, full of wonder.

"Yes," said Amy. "Let's do it!"

"Amy," said Suzi. "I'm not sure . . ."

"Mum! You can't say no to me!"

"What? Why not?"

Amy laughed. "Because I'm disabled!" she said.

Chapter 70

I've got this

It was an overnight train. The three of them had a cabin, which they could sleep in. They left on Christmas Eve, which meant that when they arrived, really early in the morning, in Scotland, it was Christmas Day.

Peter was at the station to pick them up. He was driving a vehicle none of them had seen before.

"Happy Christmas, family!" he said, getting out and hugging Amy.

"Hey, Dad!" said Amy. "You bought a version of Mum's van!"

"A slightly newer-looking version . . ." said Suzi.

"I did," said Peter, pressing a button at the back to extend the ramp. "I thought if Amy was going to be coming up to see me a bit more often, I'd better have something to drive you around in."

Amy's eyes widened. "Am I going to be coming up to see you a bit more often?"

Peter smiled. "I hope so. But that's up to you . . ."

He put his hands on the handles at the back of her chair, as if he was going to push her up the ramp. But Amy said, "That's OK, Dad. I've got this."

And wheeled herself up into the van.

Chapter 71

The biggest present ever

They drove away from the railway station. Amy and Jack, in the back of the van, watched their mum and dad, who were sitting together in the front. They weren't speaking, but it didn't seem like a bad not-speaking – more like a not-sure-what-to-say-yet type of not-speaking.

But then Suzi did say something.

"Where are we going? I thought you lived in the city centre?"

"I do. Sorry. I just wanted to show you all something before we go to my house."

Amy looked out of the window. It had clearly been snowing for a while, as all the roads and houses were covered in white, but still . . . something about where they were felt familiar.

"Dad . . ." she said. "Are we going to the Facility?"

"Maybe," he replied.

Twenty minutes later, as they were standing – Amy sitting in her chair, obviously – outside the Facility, Jack said, "Not sure why you said 'maybe' – we just were."

Peter looked at Suzi and Amy. "Is this what he's like all the time?"

They nodded.

"OK," said Peter.

"But actually, Peter," said Suzi, "I think we . . . and the kids . . . would like to maybe get to your house and start Christmas properly."

"Yes . . . I know. And I've got presents for Jack and . . . for you, Suzi . . ."

"Have you?" said Suzi, surprised.

"Yes. Under my tree, waiting."

"At least we don't have to decorate that one," said Jack.

"But," said Peter, ignoring that, "*Amy's* Christmas present is here."

He turned towards the doors of the Facility, which opened wide. Standing there was something enormous under a *lot* of wrapping paper. It looked like the biggest present ever.

"Oh! Wow!" said Amy. "Shall I go over and unwrap it?"

Her dad smiled. "I'm hoping it will unwrap for you." There was a pause. Then he turned towards the present and said more loudly, "I said, 'I'm hoping it will unwrap for you!'"

An engine sound was heard, starting up.

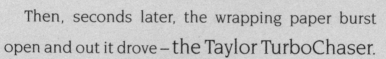

Then, seconds later, the wrapping paper burst open and out it drove – the Taylor TurboChaser.

Chapter 72

Where would you like to go today?

Only it wasn't exactly the Taylor TurboChaser.

It *was*, but it had been given an amazing upgrade! It was no longer built with fish tanks and cat flaps and banged-together trays and chimneys and wheelchairs. It was built with real car materials: aluminium and glass and steel. It was shiny and bullet-grey and sleek and streamlined – but the basic design was still the same. It still looked like the Taylor TurboChaser.

"Happy Christmas, Amy," said her dad.

"Wow!" said Amy. "The Taylor TurboChaser Mark 2!"

"Exactly! It even says so on the number plate!"

Which it did. The words TAYTURB2 became clearer as the vehicle got closer, and then stopped in front of Amy in her chair. A driver in a helmet got out. He took the helmet off. Amy recognised him as one of the drivers who had been on the track on that day two months before.

He smiled at her and handed her the helmet.

"So here's the thing, Amy," said her dad. "This is your Christmas present. It's your car. It does come with one, very specific, condition. Which is . . . you can't drive it on public roads. You *certainly* can't drive it out of here and all the way back home. *Or the* other way round."

"OK," said Amy. "So when *can* I drive it?"

"Whenever you visit me. You can come here

and drive it on the track. I will make sure the track is clear for you. Or maybe even organise some of my people to drive against you. We know you can give them quite a race!"

"Wow! Thanks, Dad! Mum, can I come up and see Dad a *lot*?"

Suzi looked at Peter, and then at Amy, and smiled. "We'll see. Yes. Maybe."

Peter smiled back.

"But meanwhile," said Amy, "can I have a go *now*?"

"Can I have a go now?" said Jack.

"Jack . . ." said Suzi. "I've told you about—"

"No, I mean it. I wasn't being sarcastic. If Amy's going to have a go now . . . well, I want a go too."

"Not just you, Jack," said Amy. "As far as I remember, the Taylor TurboChaser's got four seats, hasn't it?"

Peter looked at Suzi. Suzi shrugged. Peter looked

round at his driver, who had already gone and got three more helmets.

Then the whole family got into the TurboChaser. It was amazing inside – the seats were all black and comfortable, and there were electric windows, and heaters, and even a screen on the dashboard. But the main driving seat was still designed as if it was a wheelchair. It had the same driving controls, and all the buttons were the same.

"I've built it round your original chair," said Peter. "The Mobilcon. It's still in there, your chair, at the heart of the TurboChaser."

"Wow!" said Amy. "Although no sat nav . . . ?"

"Try the screen," said Peter.

Amy raised her eyebrows. She tapped on the screen. A sat nav logo and a map came up, glowing, accompanied by a little musical sting.

"*Hello, Amy* . . ." it said.

"Ha ha!" said Amy.

"I've programmed it to say that," said Peter proudly.

"*Ble hoffech chi fynd heddiw?*"

"Hmm, but not that," said Peter. "That's weird . . ."

"It's Welsh," said Amy.

"How do you know that?" said Suzi.

Amy smiled and punched the sat nav. It said, "*I mean, where would you like to go today?*"

Everyone looked at Amy. She didn't even have to think.

"To the race track!" she said.

"Very well," said the sat nav. "Turn left, and then . . . just drive."

"Oh, I will," said Amy, and she threw the direction lever forward. The rest of the family were thrown back in their chairs. And the Taylor TurboChaser Mark 2 sounded, it sounded – well – like the devil clearing his throat.

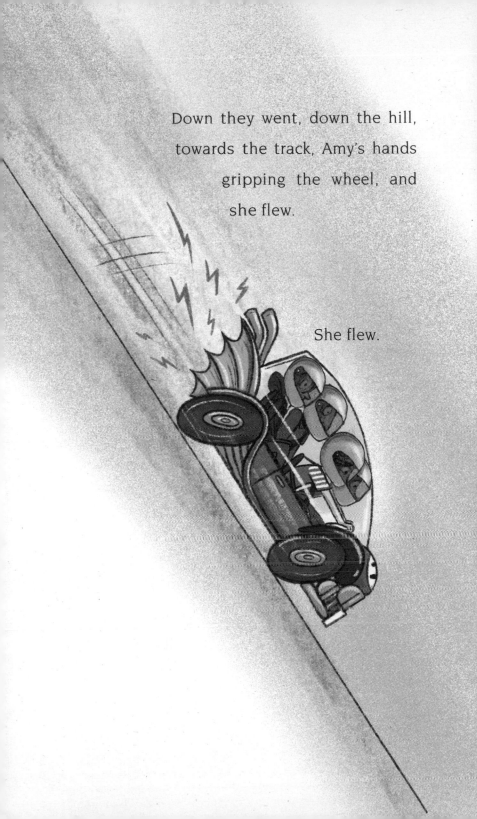

Down they went, down the hill,
towards the track, Amy's hands
gripping the wheel, and
she flew.

She flew.

Thanks to:

All the people who helped in the creation of this book. Steven Lenton, my amazing illustrator; Nick Lake, my equally amazing editor; Samantha Stewart, my — I'm going to have to use another word now — I am a writer — brilliant copy-editor; Ann-Janine Murtagh, my extraordinary — it's another adjective, but it's true — publisher; the fabulous — I'm going to stop commenting on the adjectives now, except for that comment — HarperCollins Marketing, Sales and PR team, including Geraldine Stroud, Jo-Anna Parkinson, Sally Wilks, Alex Cowan and Sam White; my inspired — oops! — designers David McDougall and Elorine Grant; Tanya Hougham the great — see — oh, I suppose that's a comment — audio-book producer; and everyone else who gets the books made and into the hands of children.

Also my homies: Morwenna Banks, Dolly Banks-Baddiel and Ezra Banks-Baddiel, who always help in numerous ways when I'm writing a book. Well, not Ezra, actually. If you want to know what he's like, see Jack. In this book.